BRIGIT, LADY OF THE IRISH OTHERWORLD
Where Goddess, Saint and Fairy Meet

BRIGIT, LADY OF THE IRISH OTHERWORLD

Where Goddess, Saint and Fairy Meet

PAULINE BREEN

MERCIER PRESS

Dedication

A Bhríghde

MERCIER PRESS
Cork
www.mercierpress.ie

© Pauline Breen, 2026

ISBN: 978-1-917453-67-7

978-1-80690-023-7 eBook

This book is sold subject to the condition that it shall not, by way of trade or otherwise, be lent, resold, hired out or otherwise circulated without the publisher's prior consent in any form of binding or cover other than that in which it is published and without a similar condition including this condition being imposed on the subsequent purchaser.

No part of this publication may be reproduced or transmitted in any form or by any means, electronic or mechanical, including photocopying, recording or any information or retrieval system, without the prior permission of the publisher in writing.

Printed and bound in the EU.

Contents

Introduction	7
The Sí and Brigit	25
The Otherworld of Ireland and Brigit	47
Death, the Otherworld and Brigit	53
Brigit's Otherworldly Abilities	78
Places of the Otherworld in Ireland are linked to Brigid	119
Connecting with Brigit as Lady of the Irish Otherworld	132
Endnotes	143
Bibliography	153
About the Author	159

Introduction

Tracing the thread of Brigit's cloak through Irish history reveals her deep and enduring connection to the Irish Otherworld. Evidence suggests that Brigit can be understood as a fairy woman or elemental spirit rooted in Ireland's pre-Celtic belief systems, long before the arrival of the first Celts. Looking back at these earlier layers of tradition uncovers another, lesser-known aspect of Brigit, one that predates both the goddess and the saint.

In Ireland, she is most often portrayed as a mother goddess or as a historical holy woman, yet these definitions do not fully contain her. Beyond them emerges a more ancient presence: Brigit as Lady of the Irish Otherworld, a figure whose essence continues to bridge the human and the divine.

To declare Brigit as a fairy woman requires examining what exactly might be meant when referring to and describing fairies in Ireland. Yeats called Ireland the land of faery – a land existing parallel to the natural world, comprising a variety of beings of various shapes and sizes. These beings referred to by Yeats include the leprechaun, the *Púca*, the *Maighdean-mhara* (mermaid), the *Leannán sídhe* and, of course, the *Bean Sí* (banshee). In addition to these commonly known beings, Farrelly lists other entities, such as the Alp-luachra, the Clurichaun, the *Fear Dearg*, *Fear Gorta* and the Grogach, among other supernatural beings.[1]

These supernatural entities fall under the broader classification of fairies, which Yeats categorised into two distinct types: solitary and trooping figures. The trooping fairies, also known as sociable fairies, are characterised by their collective behaviour and festive nature. According to traditional accounts, these beings travel in ceremonial processions mounted on white horses, whose manes are intricately braided and adorned with bells that produce a distinctive tinkling sound as they move.[2] MacKillop notes that solitary fairies may be closely associated with death. Michael Houlihan expands this classification system to include additional categories: warring fairies, malevolent fairies, fairy doctors and wise women, healing fairies and sea fairies.[3]

The term 'fairy' often conjures images of a Tinkerbell type – a minuscule, winged figure. But this image, although it readily comes to mind, primarily because of Hollywood, is not entirely accurate, nor does it cover all types of fairies. A fairy, as described by O'Brien, 'is an entity who primarily lives in the Irish Otherworld, a separate world of existence that runs parallel to ours.'[4]

These entities are described as coming in all

shapes and sizes, possessing specialised supernatural abilities that differ from one another. In traditional accounts, they do not all look the same, nor do they all have the same skills. The world of the fairies is so deeply embedded in Irish tradition that to deny or separate it from this one would be akin to having a body without a soul. It is, as Machán Mangan said, 'so intermingled that one cannot be considered without the other'.[5]

For many in Ireland, this world is tangible. It is a given for a specific cohort that humans, along with the fairies, cohabit this island. Not only is the island full of fairies in traditional belief, but it is also full of stories about them. From Munster to Ulster, many tales of fairy encounters are told across the island. As varied as the supernatural beings seem to be, the same goes for the stories told about them. Supernatural creatures from one region may be completely unknown in another, yet these beings – and the stories that contain them – share striking commonalities. Similar characteristics include their various remarkable, supernatural abilities, such as when they disappear, they go like fog, or when they speak, they have a 'silvery voice, quick and sweet'.[6] They are generally said to be kind, helpful, benevolent creatures, but can also be jealous, spiteful and downright nasty, especially when disrespected. Irish folklore documents a folk belief that they were angels who did not participate in the battle between God and Lucifer.[7] Folklore sources classify them as either benevolent or malevolent fairies. Traditional practices involved rituals designed to 'placate the bad ones and reward the good ones'.[8] These beings are traditionally associated with dancing, feasting and athletic pursuits, including hurling, football and combat. According to folklore, they function as guardians of the natural world and respond negatively to disrespect directed at themselves or the land, as well as to poor manners or dishonesty. They are primarily nocturnal entities with connections to death, and folklore identifies them as the gods and goddesses of the Tuatha Dé Danann – the divine race of Irish mythology. The Tuatha Dé Danann provides the primary connection to Brigit in her role as sovereign of the Irish Otherworld. Traditional accounts of fairy encounters consistently describe these beings as possessing specific supernatural abilities: the capacity to appear and disappear at will, to manifest into physical form, to grant wishes, to speak in tongues and to move freely between the human and Otherworld realms. Brigit demonstrates these same capabilities – appearing and disappearing at will, manifesting in physical form, granting wishes, and serving as the conduit of otherworldly inspiration to Irish poets and bards. While folklore maintains that fairies can enter the human realm, their own world remains protected by barriers that exclude humans, except those individuals considered sensitive enough to perceive their presence through sight, sound, or intuition. These beings are primarily associated with nocturnal activity – possibly due to the quieter conditions – and are consistently depicted as favouring music, dancing and feasting.

Before the arrival of the Irish Celts, the indigenous population presumably adhered to the fairy faith, the *creideamh sí*. This belief system persisted in Ireland until the eighteenth century. The following passage illustrates the traditional understanding of how humanity and the fairy realm coexisted:

> Before the triumph of modernity – sealed in Western Europe of the seventeenth century by the advent of the scientific revolution – people lived in constant interaction with a host of beings, powers and spirits who tricked us, protected us, quarrelled with us, guided us, taught us, punished us, and conversed with us … The multifarious beings taught us to share the bounty of this world with them; they taught us the gestures of reciprocity; they taught us to fear greed and accumulation. They taught us that the wealth of the plant beings, the tree beings, the water beings, soil beings, the mineral beings was not only ours, was not there for the sole purpose of satisfying our needs. They had their own reason for existing, their own requirements and their own agency. We needed to ask permission, to share, to give back, and give thanks. These very gestures made us aware that we were only one strand in an immense tapestry that wove the pattern of life on this earth.[9]

These beings mentioned by Apffel have occupied the Irish landscape and existed as otherworldly neighbours to the human population. Older generations were so accustomed to their presence, even if unseen, that they were reluctant to call them 'fairies' for fear of bad luck. As such, they often referred to them as the Other Crowd, the Good People, the Good Neighbours, the Good Folk, the Gentry or the Wee Folk.

Much like a game of draughts, the new faith of the Celts took over the fairy faith and this process of the new absorbing the old continued with the arrival of Christianity. Each one taking over the other.

Although the older ways and traditions were subsumed into the new, they did not disappear. They could not. This is the same essence as Brigit. Her spirit is contained within each of her identities. Identities of Brigit, as mentioned earlier, are goddess and saint in Ireland, but beyond Ireland, her other identities include Brigantia and Maman Brigitte. The older ways and traditions of the *creideamh sí* are especially evident at the sacred sites that dot the Irish landscape. Their presence can be detected in the legacy of Ireland's ancestors, whose belief system and collective spirit are intertwined with the land that is home to both the human race and the fairy folk.

When the Celts arrived in Ireland, they found sacred, elevated sites with established rites. With their arrival, the deities brought by the Irish Celts became associated with the revered sites. Celtic rites and customs mingled with earlier practices such as worshipping the supernatural beings of the land – the fairies. The same pattern repeated with the arrival of Christianity: Christian figures became associated with pagan sites and Christian rites and customs mingled with pre-Christian practices. The game of draughts continued. Ireland's earliest human inhabitants arrived around 7000 BC, crossing from Scotland into the northeast. The settlers took refuge in coastal areas and forests, living by hunting and fishing.[10]

These early Irish settlers held beliefs about hidden forces inhabiting the environment. As Ireland was thickly forested during this period, the population practised rituals designed to placate and control the environment, or rather, the beings believed to dwell within it who directly influenced natural phenomena. Ancient cultures commonly attributed natural phenomena to the actions of Otherworld beings. The spiritual framework of these populations is centred on nature and ancestral veneration.[11] If the custom was to conduct rituals to placate nature, ancestors and nature spirits, then there was likely some trepidation concerning these beings or fairies in traditional belief. It appears that as much as they were honoured, they were also feared. Brigit is not typically feared as much as honoured in contemporary practice. Still, her identity may have undergone such a transformation that components of her personality that her devotees feared in earlier periods have been overlooked.

The Celtic settlers who came to Ireland brought a wealth of influence that impacted the existing Irish culture. The overseas Celts migrated from various regions, bringing diverse customs and spiritual beliefs with them from their travels to their new lands. Their influences were many and included old European, Indo-European, African, Gaulish and British traditions, among others.

Although a diverse array of spiritual practices and beliefs was introduced to Ireland, the cult of Danu was particularly significant. Danu is considered the mother goddess. Various titles of the mother goddess were subsequently converted into personages in Ireland, such as Bóinn, Sionann and Brigid.[12]

Brigit's association with the mother goddess archetype is particularly evident through her symbolic connection with milk.[13]

If the Celts brought the mother goddess into Ireland, her personality likely evolved to meet the needs of the new people who settled on Irish soil. This is plausible, given the transformation of her character from a pre-Christian goddess to a Christian saint. Over time, elements of earlier belief, particularly those rooted in the fairy faith, may have been absorbed into her developing identity, reflecting the spiritual adaptation of the settlers themselves.

New settlers arrived who were not dependent on hunting and fishing. These settlers domesticated cattle and sheep and cultivated barley and wheat. Their customs and advancements in Irish society would alter earlier traditions and most probably earlier spiritual beliefs. This was the period when passage graves were constructed. As defined by Harbison, these are graves in which access to a burial chamber is gained through a passage (hence the name), both of which are covered by a round mound of earth and stone.[14] They are often erected on the top of hills or ridges, where they can be seen for miles around. It is estimated that there are some 250 passage tombs in Ireland.[15]

The construction of these passage graves on elevated sites and the role of fire in the ritual of death provide a significant link to Brigit as a fairy woman. The practice of burning the deceased before internment demonstrates the powerful role of fire held by Ireland's new settlers. Fire is the element most often associated with Brigit. What is generally not associated with Brigit in Ireland is death. However, Brigit was once closely associated with death.

Much like aspects of the goddess that were no longer recognised and arguably the old ways of the fairy faith that existed before the Celts, the new glossed over the old and, in doing so, diminished earlier belief. The old ways were pushed out to make way for the new dominant practices. Over time, the very name 'fairy' became a pejorative term, used to dismiss many characters from ancient Celtic myths, legends, sagas and folklore.[16] With the transition to Christianity, old gods and goddesses from pre-Christian Ireland became categorised as 'fairies'. The once-honoured deities were reduced in both status and power. This transformation possibly explains why fairies are also called 'wee folk', signifying small, almost childlike spirits.

The great gods of the Tuatha Dé Danann, who featured in Ireland's sagas and myths, underwent successive diminishment – from gods to kings and from kings to diminutive fairies. Figures like the Dagda became king of the *sídhe*. While kingship remains a prestigious title, it represents a human rather than divine status.

Through this process, ancient gods became mere mortals. The reduction in status appears more pronounced in the treatment of goddesses. Irish goddesses, particularly those associated with death or war, were portrayed as demonic and relegated underground with the fairies. This relegation provides evidence of Brigit's connection to the fairy folk, suggesting that she, along with other 'dark' goddesses, may have retreated underground as part of the Tuatha Dé Danann.

The nature of fairies and the fairy faith predating the Celts and Christians having been established, Brigit's place within the tapestry of Irish fairies emerges. Whether Brigit can be considered an Irish fairy queen like Áine, Clíodhna, Aoibheall or Macha remains questionable. Yet an otherworldly aspect of her identity differs from both the mother goddess and the saint – an element that remains relevant in contemporary contexts.

When examining how spiritual practices were absorbed historically, no deity in Ireland has evolved into as many different versions as Brigit. Brigit represents the definition of a liminal figure. In Ireland, she is commonly understood as straddling both pre-Christian and Christian worlds, transitioning between the roles of goddess and saint. Her liminality may have its origins between the fairy faith and pre-Christian faith, transitioning between fairy being and goddess. This remains speculation rather than fact. Houlihan also questions whether the fairy folk represented the original Aboriginal peoples, the primal occupants or nature spirits of the land.[17] These nature spirits of the land would likely have undergone a transformation in identity when either conquered by or assimilated into the spiritual systems of the arriving populations.

The passage grave functioned not only as a place of the dead, like contemporary Irish cemeteries, but as a site of continued life where the sun played a significant role.[18] Within the chambers of Newgrange, the rising sun facilitated a form of social rebirth. Through this rebirth process, the sun released the spirits of the dead into a new and socially valuable existence.[19] The sun in that process represents life, death and rebirth. Fire played a powerful role by releasing the spirit of the deceased into the Otherworld from passage graves, and within that fire resides Brigit, who held a sacred role as psychopomp. From her association with the sun and fire, she functions as a solar goddess, embodying life, death and rebirth.

At one time, all three components of life, death and rebirth were contained within every goddess and all three elements were equally acknowledged and respected. This changed with the evolving religious and spiritual landscape of Ireland. Light and continued earthly life were recognised within early goddesses, but other aspects were dismissed or vilified. Some goddesses became entirely separated from light and life and were denigrated – goddesses such as Macha or the Morrigan, for example. In neo-pagan communities, the love and light culture came into prominence, further denying the 'darker', less favourable aspects. Brigit is one such goddess who has become most typically associated with light, to the detriment of her other, darker aspects, which were arguably acknowledged in her earlier worship.

Irish fairies are said to be of the hills/*sídhe*. In the world of faery, time does not exist. There is no ugliness, sickness, age or death, but banqueting, music and dancing. Life is eternal and continues without the weight of the physical body. Fairies are said to favour the colour green or the palest of whites. These colours are also strongly associated with Brigit. Fairies are often invisible or can become so at will.[20]

They prefer to live underground. If affronted, they will retaliate by burning houses or spoiling crops. Often, fairies are depicted as benevolent, giving money or food to people experiencing poverty, providing toys for children, or counteracting the spells of witches.[21] These acts of giving to the poor and looking after children notably parallel Brigit's own attributes.

Brigit's otherworldly abilities, as found in traditional narratives, are examined in detail later; however, the above descriptions reveal an immediate connection between Brigit and the Good People. The heights of the *sídhe*/hills reflect the essence of her name, meaning 'high' or 'exalted'. The height of the hills functions both physically and metaphorically, suggesting that the banishment of the old fairy faith and the goddess beneath the earth may be more symbolic than literal. In the *sídhe*, time does not exist, which corresponds with Brigid's liminal essence and timelessness. The colours green and white are strongly associated with Brigit, both as a goddess and a saint. Wentz notes that green is the colour that nearly all the Fairy-folk of Britain and Ireland wear.[22] In the *Colloquy with Ancients*, Saint Patrick and Caeilte are talking when they are approached by a lone woman, robed in a mantle of green, with a glittering plate of yellow gold on her forehead. She said she was of the cave of Croghan. She said her name was Scothniamh/Flower-lustre, daughter of Bodhb Dearg, granddaughter of An Dagda.[23] Brigit, usually portrayed wearing the green mantle, is also connected to the Dagda as his daughter. Another tale tells of two women dressed in cloaks, one in green and one in crimson. The woman in the green cloak approaches Cúchulainn and asks him to go with her to the Plain of Delight/The Otherworld. Here, an overlap can be reasonably identified between Brigid's green mantle and the fairy-folk.

Brigit, like the fae, can appear or disappear at will, as when she appeared to the fighting Leinstermen in the Battle of Allen by materialising above them. The generous traits of the saint are evident in accounts of taking items and giving them to people experiencing poverty and providing for children. The *Leannán sídhe*, as claimed by Lady Wilde (1887), is the spirit of life and inspirer of the singer and poet.[24] This is, without doubt, recognisable in Brigit, as the superlative storyteller and goddess of poetry. Tinkling bells were also associated with poets and bards, of whom Brigit is also patroness.

There are yet more clues that link Brigit to the

fairies. Folklorist Eddie Lenihan has declared the term 'otherworldly' to mean 'closeness of land'.[25]

The very existence of fairy hills is a testament to a culture's connection with nature.[26] The fairies are indeed creatures of the outdoors, with their dwellings said to be located within the land itself. As a mother goddess expression, Brigit embodies the land. This 'closeness of land' is further reinforced through her strong water connection, most notably in the healing wells of Ireland, where she appears in both goddess and saint forms. Traditional belief held that entry to the Otherworld was possible through wells. The magical number three, which appears in fairy folklore and in Brigid's identity as triple goddess of healing, poetry and smithcraft, creates another link between the Otherworld and Brigit. An additional connection to the wee folk in her goddess form lies in her *fios*/knowledge of smithcraft. Traditional accounts state that smiths and all those adept in smithcraft belonged to the Otherworld. Beyond the colours green and white, red is associated with both the mother goddess archetype and the Otherworld. Red symbolises life, vibrancy, strength and vigour.[27] Red was given a mystical significance. In Irish, the name for red is *dearg*, which was a usual name for a god in early Ireland.[28] Brigit's connection to the colour red manifests through her association with fire, de- scriptions of flaming red hair and the white and red-eared cow that weaned the young Saint Brigid.

Otherworldly cues emerge particularly prominently in her saintly appearance. Water features centrally through her magical wells. She is linked to a red-eared cow that traditional accounts claim came from the Otherworld. Her ability to manifest proves most miraculous – not only in her physical manifestation as Saint Brigid, but also throughout her stories, where she provides endless food to people experiencing poverty without depleting her supplies. Her narratives describe transforming water into ale and manifesting lakes of milk. Music and feasting, hallmarks of the Otherworld, feature prominently in her lore as a saint, especially when hosting weary travellers or visiting clergy.

These connections between Brigit and the Otherworld represent merely a starting point. When Irish geographical landmarks, mythology, historical, archaeological and linguistic references converge, another face emerges – that of a lady of the Irish Otherworld. Given her strong Leinster affiliation, she might be claimed as a fairy woman and possibly the queen of the Leinster fairies.

Even if Brigit cannot be included on the official list of Irish fairy queens, the magical energy emanating from her remains undeniable, particularly in her miraculous and saintly stories that hint at otherworldly connections. Understanding Brigit's energy requires appreciating how each identity incorporates previous ones. With Brigit, the old always forms part of the new – each face distinct, yet containing elements of others.

Recognising Brigit as a lady of the Irish Otherworld means acknowledging the old Irish religion, honouring ancestors and venerating nature as both animate and a portal to the divine. This is her message as a fairy woman: the old faith must be preserved, the relationship with the natural world rebuilt and all sentient beings respected. Of all Brigit's faces, this otherworldly aspect offers particular guidance for contemporary concerns.

The fairy energy of Brigit represents a lesser-known dimension of this complex figure. The following pages explore this aspect through multiple lenses: her mythological and genealogical connections to the Irish *sí*; her association with the Irish Otherworld itself; her link to death in Irish mythology; the remarkable otherworldly attributes in her vast lore as goddess and saint; specific Irish locations that serve as access points to the Otherworld and connect to Brigit; and practical ways to connect with Brigit as she of the *sí*. Throughout, 'Brigit' refers to the goddess and 'Brigid' to the saint. Brigit is a deity of depth – more than the returning light at *Imbolc*, more than a saint, possibly beyond complete comprehension.

The journey ahead follows a bumpy *bóithrín* (a

narrow country road) towards the large tumulus in the distance. Listen carefully and the tunes of the Otherworld tinkle in the quiet air. The mound ahead is not what it seems. Beneath the underlayer reside the *sí*. And within the *sí*, is she, Brigit.

1

THE SÍ AND BRIGIT

The *sí/sithe/sídhe*, the Irish Otherworld, death and fairies are thoroughly entwined, so much so that it is difficult to separate them without constant overlap. Within all this overlapping, Brigit arguably appears as a common element throughout.

For clarification, fairies in Irish are *sí*. In Old Irish, they are *sídh*, which originally meant a mound.[1]

For simplicity, the spelling *sí* will denote the fairy folk and *sídhe* will designate mounds/hills (plural spelling of *sidhe*). *Suí* is the Irish word for sitting, so places, hills and mounds could also be considered seating grounds where the deceased are seated/buried. In considering Brigit as a lady of the Irish Otherworld, the starting point is the *sí*, as the *sídhe* have been identified as the starting point to journey towards the Otherworld. It was to the *sídhe* that fairies, the fairy faith, gods and goddesses of Ireland either retreated or were banished.

The *sí* are probably the most distinctive aspect of Irish mythology and are unique to Ireland. The *creideamh sí*, despite having so little verification or documented evidence, is perhaps the most untouched aspect of native Irish history. Nothing has been amended or altered because there is so little written record of the megalithic people and their culture that exists. Folktales gathered by the National Folklore Collection and stories documented by folklorists have helped keep evidence of it alive. Yet, despite the paucity of written records and the significant passage of time, mention of fairies persists in modern Ireland. To this day, stories of the wee folk circulate and customs are still practised to placate, honour, or ward them off.

Evidence of fairy belief in Ireland appears when somebody spots a comb or brush outside a window of their home and dares not pick it up in case it belongs to the *Bean Sí*, or when construction workers, in agreement with the government, circumvent a fairy rath rather than build a road over it. Contained within these observations is proof that the fairy faith still exists in Ireland, even if it remains somewhat 'hush hush'. This secrecy stems mainly from fear of ridicule for holding such beliefs.

The *sí* are said to be the divine race, the Tuatha Dé Danann. From the National Folklore Collection: 'The numerous moats that are seen throughout Ireland are supposed to be the homes of the fairies. According to tradition, the fairies are an ancient and magical race known as the Tuatha Dé Danann. When they were defeated in battle, they changed themselves into little people and hid in the hills.'[2]

Most prominent within this divine tribe is

Brigit's father, the king of the *sí*, the Dagda. Brigit is genealogically connected to the Tuatha Dé Danann through the Dagda. He is also said to have a son, Finnbhearra, who is the Fairy King of Connacht. Finnbhearra is mentioned in the *Agallamh na Seanórach* and identified as the youngest son of the Dagda. If he is a fairy king, it seems feasible that his sister Brigit could be a fairy queen. Yet Brigit is never mentioned as a fairy queen or fairy goddess despite her genealogical roots and sibling connection to the *sí*.

The Tuatha Dé Danann arrived in Ireland at *Bealtaine*, one of the four major turning points of the year, alongside *Imbolc*, *Lughnasa* and *Samhain*. At this mid-turn point, the old and new fuse. This energy of old and new coming together aligns with Brigit's nature. At these pivotal moments, tradition holds that the barriers between the two worlds are lowered, making visitation to both highly probable. At *Bealtaine* and *Samhain* in Ireland, as the seasons change, the fairies are believed to be on the move across the land. Sightings at these times are commonly reported, especially at night.

The Tuatha Dé Danann, the sacred tribe, arrived from the north, surrounded by a mist.[3]

Before arriving in Ireland, they lived in the four cities of Falias, Gorias, Murias and Findias. Here, they learned their secret knowledge and skill from four wizards.[4] They possessed an immense knowledge of metal, which is strongly connected to Brigit. Brigit, as a triplicate goddess, presides over smithwork as well as healing and poetry. Once settled in Ireland, the Tuatha Dé demanded a division of the kingdom from the Firbolgs, who were the pre-Celtic folk of Ireland. The Tuatha Dé Danann remained in control of Ireland until the arrival of the Milesians. When the Milesians landed, they demanded immediate battle or the surrender of the land.[5] Once defeated, the survivors of the Tuatha Dé Danann retreated into the hills (*Sídhe*) to become a fairy folk, and the Milesians (the Goidels or Scots) became the ancestors of Ireland. The *sídhe*, described as marvellous the underground palaces full of strange things.[6] They became the home of the divine, of Ireland's old gods and goddesses, among whom Brigit holds her place.

The Tuatha Dé Danann were supernatural in character, possessing extraordinary powers, divine and unfailing food and drink, and a mysterious and beautiful abode.[7] Ó Duinn describes the Tuatha Dé Danann as having three great treasures: the *Faeth Fíadhe*, the supernatural cloak of invisibility; the *Flea Ghoibheann*, the supernatural drink of Goibniu, the blacksmith of the Tuatha Dé Danann, that prevented death and old age; and the *Muca Mhanannáin*, the pigs of Manannán Mac Lir, that, even though they were killed and cooked today, they would be alive and kicking the following day.[8] Indeed, these three great treasures of the Tuatha Dé Danann feature prominently in Brigid's lore as a Saint, highly suggestive of the Otherworld, mainly due to her ability to multiply food and drink for people experiencing poverty and her guests. The Tuatha Dé Danann were nature deities associated with growth, light, agriculture, fertility, culture, crafts and war.[9] All of these descriptions are also evident in the goddess Brigit, including her association with war. However, within the stories of Saint Brigid, all of them feature, *except* for war.

The Tuatha Dé Danann are the ancient deities of the Celts of Ireland. But there may be, among them, older divinities from the megalithic period.[10] The Tuatha Dé Danann are considered divine due to their intelligence and the excellence of their knowledge. They were portrayed as patrons and bestowers of things that involved social prestige, such as the arts, skills and even kingship itself.[11] Brigit is often described as a goddess of the arts, specifically poetry and the spoken word.

Even though the Tuatha Dé Danann are considered divine, they are also regarded as fairy kings and queens, and yet fairies of a different order from those of ordinary tradition. They are fairies or sprites with corporeal forms, endowed with immortality.[12] If this tribe, to whom Brigit belongs, can be considered as a tribe of fairy kings and queens, then the term fairy queen could reasonably apply to Brigit. Additionally, if these beings of the Otherworld are 'endowed with immortality', this reflects the ultimate essence of Brigit, which is born and reborn time and again. In her consistent rebirthing, she reveals her depth and many faces in her various personas, such as Maman Brigitte and Brigantia. Giving credence to her otherworldly nature perhaps provides a fresh trilogy in an Irish context, away from maiden, mother, crone, but rather: Fairy Queen, Goddess and Saint.

Mythologically, the Tuatha Dé Danann are gods of light and good. They can control natural phenomena to produce abundant harvests. As one of the Tuatha Dé, Brigit is revered as the goddess of light at *Imbolc*, marking the return of life to the land. The Tuatha Dé Danann also inhabit fairy palaces, enjoy rare feasts and love-making and have their own music and minstrelsy.[13]

The palaces to which the Tuatha Dé Danann retired when conquered by the race of Mil were hidden beneath the earth, in hills, under ridges, more or less elevated.[14] The elevation of these hills reflects her title *brig*. Her name *brig* means 'most high', which possibly derives from the fact that many hills in Ireland were called *Brigh* or *Brí*.[15] Gods (and goddesses) were frequently associated with heights.

They were also very much associated with and venerated at specific natural landmarks in Ireland. Gods worshipped at mounds, dwelling or revealing themselves there, still lingered in the haunted spots; they became fairies, or were associated with the dead buried in the mounds, as fairies also have been.[16]

There is much speculation about whether the *sí* existed before the Tuatha Dé Danann joined them underground or whether the Tuatha Dé Danann created the *sí* into being once underground. It is said that when the Tuatha Dé Danann defeated the Firbolgs, they either retreated underground or went off to the west.[17] Either way, beneath the earth, the divine and the fairy became assimilated and associated with fertility and abundance. As the Celtic mother goddess, Brigit is most closely associated with fertility and abundance, and arguably embodies the divine and fairy realms. In the *Book of Armagh*, the *sí* are described as gods of the earth, or *dei terreni*, who control the ripening of crops and the milk-giving of cows. Once more, an obvious connection emerges between the fairy and the goddess Brigit. The traditions surrounding milk-giving and milk production continued into her veneration as the Christian Saint Brigid. In Christian art, Saint Brigid is frequently depicted with her white, red-eared otherworldly cow.

Brigit is deeply rooted in the Tuatha Dé Danann,

both in her genealogy and mythology, and to a lesser extent, in her connection to death, which was seen as a natural passage for mortals to gain entry into the *sídhe*.[18] Brigit is primarily regarded as a goddess of rebirth, representing the returning light and new life. But there is also a connection between her and death. Not only as mother goddess in which death and life are natural components – one is dependent upon the other – but also in her role as psychopomp.

Why would divine gods and goddesses take on a new identity? The evidence suggests that the fairy faith of Ireland and the goddess cult before Christianity were both assimilated and then diluted to pave the way for the new monotheistic faith of Christianity. MacCulloch asserts that the victory of the Milesians over the Tuatha Dé Danann can be seen as a triumph of Christianity over paganism. 'The new faith of Ireland, not the people, conquered the old gods.'[19]

It is possible that in pre-Christian and pre-Celtic Ireland, the *Creidimh sí* was alive and well. Saint Fiacc's poem on the life of Saint Patrick states that the 'Tuatha adored the Sidhi' before the coming of Patrick. The fairy faith was a highly complex religious system. According to Ó Duinn, 'it was above all a fertility cult, concerned with food production, health, protection, good harvests, children, large herds of cattle, sheep and pigs'.[20] In reality, the fairy faith was about survival. When the Celts landed on Irish shores, worship of the divine feminine would not have been alien to the native people. They presumably invoked and placated nature spirits to ensure the fecundity of crops, good weather, and ultimately, survival. Over time, there was a need to preserve good relationships with the goddess and the Tuatha Dé Danann.[21]

With the transition to Christianity, the task of scribing old Irish mythology fell into the capable but biased hands of Christian monks. In recording the old mythology, they demoted the once highly revered gods and heroes into mortal kings. These kings were buried in round, flat-topped, manmade barrows, or hillocks explicitly built to commemorate the mortal king or ruler.[22] Old gods, once worshipped at these mounds, became fairies or were associated with the dead buried within them. Either way, divine gods and goddesses that once held the highest prestige were demoted from their sacred status and merged with these earthly structures. If gods were worshipped at natural landmarks in Ireland, this would equally apply to goddesses, who were intrinsically tied to particular geographical places and intimately identified with the land itself.

While there is ample evidence to suggest Brigid is a woman of the *sídhe*, she is never mentioned in this context. Her *sídhe* connections are overlooked, effectively excluding her from recognition as a fairy queen. Yet she could hold this title and claim dominion over Leinster, in keeping with other fairy queens of Ireland who rule specific territories.

How is a fairy queen defined? According to O'Brien, queens of the *sídhe* are believed to be the memories of goddesses from ancient tribes.[23] Irish fairy queens often display both goddess and fairy characteristics.[24] If fairy queens are often memories of goddesses, then this surely applies to Brigit. The term 'fairy' was a reduction in status and a negative term, intended to belittle. Yet Brigit escaped this title and its accompanying demotion. This may be because she was elevated from beneath the mounds up into Christianity as a saint, rather than being downgraded. Other goddesses did not make the cut and were almost damned to hell. As Brigit rose to prominence within the Christian faith, she became closely associated with light. Her less favourable attributes of death remained below the earth along with the other goddesses. Meanwhile, those goddesses who did become fairy queens had the 'light' stripped from them, becoming associated exclusively with darkness.

The most well-known goddesses considered to be fairy women in Irish mythology are Áine, Aoibheall, Clíona, Úna and Macha, who is also considered an Otherworld wife.[25] Common capabilities flow through each of these fairy queens and Brigit. Áine is known as a fairy goddess of both Leinster and Munster, specifically in Louth and Limerick. Like Brigit, Áine is said to possess the gifts of healing, poetry and music.[26] She is often conflated with Danu, the mother goddess of the Tuatha Dé Danann, as was Brigit.[27] Aoibheall is associated with county Clare in the West. Like any good fairy woman, she has the ability to put 'a druid covering' over someone, rendering them invisible. She also has the gift of prophecy. In the battle of *Cluantarbh*, she forewarned Dubhlaing and Murchadh to leave the battle or else they would die. They did not heed her warning and so they died. She also possessed a golden harp, which echoes the Dagda's magic harp. It was said that whoever heard the playing of that harp would not live long after.[28] Úna was married to Brigit's brother, the king of the fairies, Finnbhearra. Úna is associated with Galway as well as Tipperary. Macha is associated with Ulster. Of all the provinces, only Leinster lacks a fairy queen among those mentioned. This notable absence suggests that Leinster's fairy sovereignty may indeed belong to Brigit, particularly given her strong connections to this province.

Some Irish fairy queens also feature the number three in their mythologies, such as Aoibheall, the Fairy Queen of Clare and Clíona, the Fairy Queen of Cork. Aoibheall is one of three fairy women travelling among various *sidhe* who light three candles on *Cnoc*

Firinne to welcome a king.[29] Cliodhna, goddess of the Irish Otherworld, has three magical birds that eat apples from the Otherworld and possess healing powers.[30] Brigit, too, has the number three energy surrounding her as a triple goddess of poetry, healing and smithcraft.

Some fairy queens also reference the sun. Áine is associated with the sun or fire and Aoibheall is from the Old Irish meaning spark or flame.[31] Brigit is associated with the returning sun and light at *Imbolc*.

It would appear that goddesses who were fairy women were known to have had human loves and to have children in human family lines, giving them motivation to follow those family lines and mourn over their death.[32] Brigit qualifies in this aspect. Her love was Bres, the mortal king, and together they had a son, Ruadán.

It was not unusual for kings to mate with the sovereign goddess. The sacral kingship among the Celts was concerned with the fertility of the land, as well as with maintaining peace and prosperity, and preserving the order of the universe.[33] In the lore of Brigit, she is the sovereign goddess of the weak-livered and temporary king Bres, who literally brought Éire and her people to their knees. Bres came to the kingship by happenstance and by the misfortune of his predecessor Nuada, who lost an arm in battle. The Tuatha Dé Danann had a law that only a man in perfect shape could rule them. Folk looked to Bres the beautiful to be their king. His good looks were viewed as a sign of the good luck he would bestow upon them and their land. But this would not be the case. Once in power, he increased taxes on the Irish people which resulted in misery. But Bres' rule could only last as long as he had the support of the sovereign goddess. His reign in this manner would be short-lived.

Finally, animals and the colours red and white are typical in fairy queen mythologies. Áine takes the form of a red mare who travels around Lough Gur. Clíona, who is sister to Aoibheall, is said to be able to turn Aoibheall into a white cat, and Úna, Fairy Queen of Tipperary, is a shapeshifter who sometimes appears as a white cow.[34] Saint Brigid's 'companion' is an otherworldly white cow with red ears.

Brigit's genealogical connection to the Tuatha Dé Danann is also through her grandfather *Bilé*, who as psychopomp, transported souls of the dead to the Otherworld via the water.[35] Her genealogical connection to the Tuatha Dé Danann is mostly through her father, The Dagda.[36] The Dagda is one of the most renowned gods of the Tuatha Dé Danann. He is identified with the sky or sun and is regarded as solar, provident and life-producing. These qualities are also to be seen in his daughter Brigit. The Dagda exists in the land of the living by day, but in that of the dead by night, yet bridges these two worlds.[37] He is a bridge and his daughter Brigit is a bridge. It would seem that The Dagda has as many names as Brigit. He is sometimes called *Eochaidh*, 'horseman', and under this name was also known as *Ollathair*, 'father of all'. He is also known as *Ruadh Ró-fheassa*, 'beautiful fire and ruddy one of much wisdom'.[38] This fire connection directly parallels Brigit's own dominion over the element of fire. In a medieval text, he is a leader of the Tuatha Dé Danann and promises to assist them against their enemies by shaking the mountains, draining the lakes and bringing showers of fire. As a result, the Tuatha Dé Danann called him the 'good god'. Although the Dagda was viewed as an important god of the pagans, he was not the ultimate god the father.[39] He is most renowned for his role as hospitaller or *Briugu* (cognate of Brig). As such, he is, much like the *sí* and much like Brigit, linked to fertility and abundance. His cauldron was one of the four treasures brought to Ireland by the Tuatha Dé Dananan. The Dagda's cauldron is what mostly comes to mind when we think of the Dagda, making him the hospitallier *par excellence*. His role as hospitaller or *Briugu* was the highest rank within the farming class.[40] This made him an important deity for the agricultural class in society, which Brigit as goddess and Brigid as saint was also.

In addition to never having a dry cauldron, he never had unfailing swine. Pigs were especially revered and venerated as an essentially otherworldly magical animal.[41] One was always living, the other was ready for cooking. Dagda always had a vessel of ale and three trees laden with fruit. He was renowned for his generosity, a trait also characteristic of Saint Brigid.[42]

The Dagda was a powerful leader who instilled a sense of security and inspiration. He wielded a great club, or a mace that could kill with one end and resurrect with another. He is, as such, a dual figure in his ability to kill and resurrect. He is, therefore, not only generous in life but linked, too, to death.

According to *De Gabail in t-Sida, the taking of the Sidhe*, when the Tuatha Dé Danann went into the *sídhe* having been defeated by the Milesians, the earth reacted. No sooner had the Tuatha Dé Danann retreated underground than the harvest and milk (*ith agus blicht*) failed. The Milesians had to ask the king of the *sídhe*, the Dagda, for help in restoring the crops, which he, as the good god, graciously provided.[43] It was agreed that humans would give to the *Daoine Sidhe*, the *sí* people, a portion of their crops and milk in return for the assurance that their land and livestock would flourish. In this case, the Dagda, as a member of the Tuatha, the community of the goddess, has magical power over cows. This animal would become central to Brigit's own mythology.

Many of Dagda's characteristics are most suggestive of the Otherworld. Otherworldly beings can be defined as possessing the ability to wield magic, exhibit cunning and scheming, and have the capacity to shapeshift or manifest into something or someone else. The assimilation of the divine gods and goddesses with fairies becomes evident when the Dagda is described as being 'a god of wixardr'.[44] Reputed for many things, including being a generous king, a stable provider for his people and kind-hearted, he was also very much a trickster. This mischievousness and trickery are also to be found regularly in the lore of Saint Brigid. The otherworldly scheming side of the Dagda comes through in several of his myths. In one such myth, this aspect is evident in how he came to father his son, Oengus. The Dagda had a desire for relations with Bóinn, who was married to Elcmar. Determined to remove Elcmar from the picture, so that he can have his way with Bóinn, the Dagda sends Elcmar on an errand. The Dagda uses his canny ways and magic to cause nine months to pass in the space of a single day, where the sun stands still.[45] He ensures that Elcmar will never experience hunger or thirst during this time. The Dagda and Bóinn unite and the child Oenghus is conceived, gestated and born on the same day. Elcmar returns oblivious to the situation.[46]

This side to him is seen once more when he is in service to the unjust king Bres. The Dagda is significantly reduced in status when working for Bres as a manual labourer. Legend goes that the Dagda was threatened with illegal satire by Crídenbél unless he handed over the three best bits of his evening meal. For a man his size, every morsel after a long day's physical work is essential. Oengus advises him to outsmart Crídenbél. Oengus gives the Dagda three pieces of gold, which the Dagda offers to Crídenbél. As soon as Crídenbél swallows them, he dies. Bres quickly accuses the Dagda of murdering Crídenbél. The Dagda proves his innocence by providing evidence that Crídenbél swallowed the gold that killed him. 'He swiftly turns the tables and accuses Bres himself of being a liar.' For a king to be accused of telling untruths would be detrimental to his rule. In addition, Oengus encourages the Dagda to take a single heifer as payment for his work, which amuses Bres. When the Dagda achieves victory, the single heifer will call to her calf and the other cows will follow, which means he will claim all the cattle of the Tuatha Dé Danann, making him the 'herdsman of the herdsmen', counting his cattle in hundreds of hundreds.[47] The heifer will restore to the Tuatha all their cattle given over to the Fomorians, thus restoring fertility and prosperity.

Brigit's father was an all-rounder, skilled in many

arts and even in trickery, which Brigit most presumably inherited. The Dagda was skilled in poetry, wisdom, and, as mentioned above, wizardry. Kelly mentions the anvil of the Dagda, which suggests he had a blacksmithing skill, too, which was primarily regarded as an otherworldly skill.[48] A skill that his daughter, Brigit, would excel in. Music and feasting surround the lore of the Dagda. These are most suggestive of the Otherworld. Dagda's harp, it is said, can change seasons. His harp can lull his enemies into a sleep that enables him and the Tuatha Dé Danann to escape, taking his heifer, her calf and all the other cows of Ireland with them. The colour red, which is also suggestive of the Otherworld is found in the Dagda.[49] He is said to have red hair and to be a red man of knowledge.[50] The number three features prominently in Irish folklore and is especially associated with the fairy folk, as seen in the connection of three to the fairy queens. The number three is also related to the Dagda. He only answers a question after being asked his name by a Fomorian princess for the third time.[51] He creates three rivers. The three sons of the Dagda mentioned in *Lebor Gabála Erenn* include Oengus, Aedh and Cermait. In *Cormac's glossary*, he is said to have three daughters, all named Brigid.

The *Aos* sí inhabit the hollow hills throughout Ireland – sacred mounds which, according to the *Book of Leinster (De Gabáil int Sída – The Taking of the Sídhe),* the Tuatha Dé Danann took as dwelling-places when they descended underground. These places are still highly visited and considered sacred even today in modern Ireland: *Newgrange, Sliabh na mBan, Sí mór, Sí beag, Cnoc Áine, Lough Gur, Cnoc Sí Una, Carraig Chlíona* – to name but a few. The names themselves reveal their inhabitants: nearly all contain either 'Sí' or the names of goddesses, marking them as doorways between worlds.

So who exactly were/are the *sí*? They were the fairy folk, unique to Ireland, unique to the land of *Banba*, of fair women and Ériu from whom Ireland derived her name. They are said to have dwelt 'in every stream of water, in every glen, in every cairn, in every fairy ring, in every field and in the very soul of the ancient breed of Celtic origin'.

According to tradition, the children of the ancient gods, both visible and invisible, were intertwined in a dream-like reality that underlay every aspect of life. Because of them, Irish soil was literally soaked in the supernatural.[52]

They have a connection to the ancient gods and goddesses of Ireland, if not themselves, and they have a specific connection to death. MacCulloch says, 'Fairies, in some respects, are ghosts of the dead'.[53] The Irish tradition of fairies was rooted in the idea that the community of the dead lived on in their burial chambers, hollow hills, or ancient monuments.

For the Celts, the community encompassed both the living and the dead. Ó Duinn notes that for the Celts, life on earth was a temporary exile from the true, undifferentiated, group-life somewhere beyond the veil. Departed souls, who were worshipped as a collective, were believed to be responsible for all the good things and bad things in life. Abundance, fertility, reproduction and victory in war are all derived from those now living beyond the veil. Hence, where the ancestors once dwelt was the most holy spot in the world.[54] The tumulus or dwelling was considered to be inhabited by the spirit of the noble dead for a definite period, and it was believed that there was a supernatural passageway from it to the Otherworld. The inside of the tumulus was considered very sacred.[55]

The mythic beings of the mounds were also understood to be a kind of spiritual community whose nature was on a different plane to that of the human race. 'They could appear to people at will and provide glittering visions of their existence.' At some stage, the Otherworld communities were assimilated into the lore of the living dead and from this evolved the *sí* people of general Irish tradition.[56]

It appears that the *sí*, the Tuatha Dé Danann and Brigit overlap, blend, and are, as a result, irrevocably interconnected. Our divinities, once connected to the natural landscape of Ireland, were banished beneath the earth. Brigit, along with the other gods and goddesses, retreated underground with the rest of her tribe. Retreated but not gone. Driven underground with the advent of Christianity, she, amongst all the other gods and goddesses, took her seat in her new abode. And here she continues to dwell. At nighttime, when the rest of the world sleeps, the *sí* step out beyond the boundaries. At seasonal turning points like *Samhain* and *Bealtaine*, the sí are known to enter our world and wreak havoc brazenly. Yet this hostility was not always present. MacCulloch tells us that fairies ceased helping humanity when humans abandoned them for Christianity.[57] But Brigit did not abandon humanity. Not she of the *sí*, not the queen of the Leinster fairies. This lady of the Irish Otherworld continues her ancient work of helping humanity, as she has always done. She evolves with the times, transforming as humanity's needs shift. Brigit is the supreme shapeshifter – from Celtic mother goddess to Christian saint, from Maman Brigitte to Brigantia. When humanity requires it, she steps through the veil and manifests in new forms. This ability to endlessly transform while maintaining her essence is both divine and otherworldly – the very power that marks her as a true lady of the Irish Otherworld.

To discover Brigit in her fairy form requires a journey to the *sídhe* – those sacred mounds that shelter her alongside our ancient divinities and ancestors. These gateways between worlds dot the island of Ireland spectacularly, each one a threshold demanding respect. First, locate the mound. Then knock and await permission. Only then may one step across that ancient boundary. The *sídhe* is where every journey to Ireland's glorious Otherworld begins.

2

THE OTHERWORLD OF IRELAND AND BRIGIT

In Irish manuscripts, the Otherworld has many names: *Tír-na-nóg* (Land of Youth), *Tír-Innambeó* (Land of the Living), *Tír-lairngire* (Land of Promise), *Tír N-aill* (Other Land), *Mag már* (Great Plain), *Mag Mell* (The Happy Plain).[1]

'The Heaven-World of the ancient Celts, unlike that of the Christians, was not situated in some distant, unknown region of planetary space, but here on our own earth ... Sometimes it was a subterranean world entered through caves, or hills, or mountains, and inhabited by many races and orders of invisible beings, such as demons, shades, fairies, or even gods. It can be accessed through the portals that exist in our world.'[2]

These places were marvellous underground palaces where life continued blissfully. Rather than a single continuous location, it is a series of interconnected places.[3] In stories, the Otherworld is described as an island or a series of islands off the coast of Ireland, generally hidden from mortal sight.[4] It is nearly always portrayed as a bright and beautiful world. It is a pleasant place with delectable food, and where time is known to stand still. It is an island surrounded by a revolving wall of fire with an opening that allows us a glimpse inside. Inside, we see attractive people dressed in beautiful clothing, drinking ale from golden goblets, accompanied by lovely music.[5]

The Otherworld is where sickness and decay are unknown. It is a land of primaeval innocence where the pleasures of love are untainted by guilt. Its women are numerous and beautiful, and they alone inhabit some of the regions, so that it becomes literally *Tir inna mBan*, the land of women. It is filled with enchanting music from bright-plumaged birds, from the swaying branches of the otherworld tree, from instruments which sound without being played, and from the very stones. And it has an abundance of exquisite food and drink and magic vessels of inexhaustible plenty.[6] The concept of 'inexhaustible plenty' flows directly from the Dagda's cauldron into Saint Brigid's miracles of abundance.

Goddesses of the Otherworld are generally beautiful and young. They are so lovely as to entice mortals from the natural world to theirs.[7] Women persuaded Irish figures such as Conla and Bran to the land of women and girls. Clíona, as she appeared to Tadhg, was beautiful. Brigit is also generally portrayed as a maiden-like, virginal and eternally youthful figure. She is typically kept youthful to coincide with her association with *Imbolc*, arguably the maiden of the Sabbats.

This underground world of the *sí*-folk was divided into districts or kingdoms, each under the rule of a different fairy king or queen, just as the upper world of mortals.[8]

Sometimes it subsumes the Mediterranean concept of the underworld, i.e the realm of the dead.[9] Anne Ross describes the Otherworld of Ireland as both 'sensual and materialistic'.[10] The Celts had a strong religious belief about the continued existence of a person after death and the cheerful nature of the Otherworld. Materialism that was part of the everyday existence for the Celts was also to be found in the Otherworld. Their graves were equipped with the articles considered necessary for the journey to the Otherworld. Upon arrival, a great feast awaited and ale brewed by the famous blacksmith Goibniu.[11] Pigs were killed and eaten, yet they would miraculously reappear the following day. This magical, or rather miraculous, ability to create abundance from nothing would feature strongly in the life of Saint Brigid.

Celtic beliefs in the Otherworld as a western island are probably derived from the Greeks. The source was probably the Greek colony of Marseilles. Navigators passed through here *en route* to the western regions, and it was a vital contact point in trade and other matters with the Gauls. The Gauls were influenced by Greek philosophy. These ideas spread to the Celts in Britain, who were influenced by the culture of the Gaulish Celts.[12] The Otherworld transcends all spatial definition. It can be reached through passage graves, or by boat across the sea, or by a lake or cave, through water, wells, magic mists, or sudden insight.[13] Insight or knowledge of the Otherworld was generally gleaned by artists or poets, of whom Brigit is patroness. One entrance to the Otherworld was said to be through the Lake of Cruachain.[14]

Water holds deep associations with the goddess and Brigit, as both goddess and saint, is intrinsically connected to wells throughout Ireland and Europe. These wells remain active sites of devotion where prayers and offerings to Brigid continue. Marija Gimbutas notes that devotees of Brigid perform ring dances around wells and menhirs to evoke her powers.[15] These fairy ring dances possibly served to connect devotees directly with her otherworldly spirit. When pilgrims visit these wells today and invoke Brigid, perhaps they invoke her of the *Sí*, the well woman of the Otherworld. Brigit by no means had sole jurisdiction over death in Ireland. This role that she held with death in pre-Christian Ireland, and arguably in the Old religion, is a role that is often overlooked. The lord of the dead in Ireland was Donn, which means dark or black one. He inhabits an island off south-west Ireland, known as

Tech Duinn, which is reachable through Bull Rock, a rocky formation with an archway through which the sea flows. It lies off the shore of the Beara Peninsula. The fourteenth-century Metrical Dindshenchas describes that souls go there to Donn and he is one of the leaders of the Gaelic people when they first came to Ireland. However, he did not reach Ireland but drowned near the rock bearing his name.[16] The house of Donn was the assembly place for the dead before they began the journey to the Otherworld.[17]

The Otherworld in Ireland was as much a reality as the living world for the poets, artists, academics and scholars of Ireland. Indeed, Brigit, as a goddess, was the goddess for all poets and scholars. The Otherworld is frequently mentioned by writers of old, as well as modern artists and folklorists. Their works often express their sense of wonderment, fascination, at times trepidation, but mostly *grá* (love) for this parallel realm. The fae folk can enter our world at will, but entering their world is for the select few humans who are either allured by lust, invited, or possess the second sight. Yeats frequently warned of the perils of entering fairy territory in his poems. What is perceived as the most beautiful, harmonious place is altogether an entirely different experience for anyone who enters uninvited or for anyone who hasn't arrived naturally through the most acceptable entry system, death.

Brigit's connection to death in Ireland – and possibly to Ireland as it once was – reveals how she played a darker and more sombre role that allowed her to not only gain entry to the Irish Otherworld, but perhaps even to have dominion there as a conceivable otherworldly fairy woman.

3

DEATH, THE OTHERWORLD AND BRIGIT

Old European goddesses that came to Ireland with the Celts embodied death, birth and rebirth. All three aspects were venerated and respected as interconnected and mutually dependent – one could not exist without the others. Contemporary understanding tends to categorise goddesses into distinct groups: those associated with light, birth and life, versus those linked to darkness, death and war. While individual goddesses representing the Great Mother may display more pronounced aspects of war, death, or life-giving properties, within each face of the Divine Mother, birth, death and rebirth all exist to varying degrees.

Over time, goddesses have been reduced to single aspects of their divinity, with other dimensions diminished or ignored. In Ireland, Brigit is most typically venerated for her life-giving qualities and the return of light at *Imbolc*. Similarly, in Irish folklore, the original death goddesses were the *Cailleach* and the *Bean Sí*.[1] Perhaps these goddesses are not separate identities, but somewhat different aspects of the same goddess, located at opposite ends of the continuum.

Brigit of Ireland is neither a death goddess nor a fairy ruler of death. That role belongs to Donn, the old fairy ruler of death whose passage to the Otherworld lies off Dursey Island. The waters there are in the territory of the *Cailleach Bhéarra*, who merits consideration in this chapter as a fairy figure and as a possible other face of Brigit. Some believe the *Cailleach* and Brigit are different aspects of the same spirit on opposite ends of the spectrum. Others view this connection as entirely inconceivable. While no definitive answer exists, all possibilities merit exploration.

Death is the most natural entrance to the *sídhe*. Brigit is connected to the *sídhe* through her mythology and genealogy. What remains to be explored is how death features within the character of Brigit of Ireland. If death can be linked to Brigit, it could be argued that she has access to, if not command over, the Otherworld.

Let us explore death in the makeup of Brigit. For clarification, Brigit, as a death goddess or lwa within the Vodou pantheon, is represented by the personality of Maman Brigitte. Evidence suggests that Maman Brigitte is a fusion of Brigit of Ireland and the African goddess Oya, reflecting the complex cultural exchanges that occurred in Haiti between various populations during the colonial period. Maman Brigitte presides predominantly over death and dwells in the cemetery. The current perspective views Brigit as both the Celtic mother goddess figure and the Christian Saint Brigid, examining their relationship to death, particularly in the Irish context.

The Celts regarded death as merely an interruption in a long life, a stage between one life and another.[2] In the Otherworld, time as we know it does not exist. It is, as Croker says, a circular dimension leading to the sacred world of the Heroes, of the immortal beings of the *sídhe*.[3] For the Celts, death was just a threshold to the Otherworld, which in itself was a world that was a passage to other, innumerable states of being, in an eternal metamorphosis, with no end, no time.[4] Metamorphosis is a word that encapsulates the essence of Brigit. Both research and tradition portray her as a spirit, an energy in constant evolution, intimately bound to the cycles of death and rebirth. Rebirth cannot occur without death, and Brigit, as a prominent member of the Tuatha Dé Danann, exemplifies the divine capacity to generate new life. This creative power appears almost hereditary, for as the daughter of the Dagda, she remains inseparable from his cauldron of rebirth.

Like Dian Cecht, the great physician of the Tuatha Dé Danann who restored fallen warriors by immersing them in healing waters, Brigit too embodies renewal and restoration. Water and healing are central to her nature, qualities reflected in her identity as mother goddess and in the countless wells across Ireland dedicated to her as both goddess and saint. Death, in this context, functions not as an end but as a threshold, a portal to the Irish Otherworld that lies at the heart of Brigit's mystery.

The *Cailleach*

The treatment of Brigit and death begins by looking to the opposite end of youth and rebirth, to the hag, the *Cailleach*, as perhaps the opposite side to Brigit. Brigit is generally regarded as dualistic, claimed in Ireland to be either a Celtic goddess or a Christian saint. In both of these personages, she is most often portrayed as a maiden-like, virginal and youthful figure. Perhaps her dualistic nature as goddess and saint could also symbolise life and death, maiden and hag, Brigit and the *Cailleach*? In Scotland, it is a more commonly held viewpoint that the *Cailleach* is the same deity as Brigid. This viewpoint is also held in Ireland. 'Imprisoned for the winter but transformed at winter's end, the *Cailleach* emerges at *Imbolg* (1 February) as Brigid, the bountiful goddess of spring.[5]

Whether these figures represent the same entity or merely share similarities deserves examination. Notable commonalities exist between them. Both have strong associations with Leinster – Brigit's original territory in Ireland, where the *Cailleach* is known as *Cailleach Laigean*, the 'Witch of Leinster'. While this geographical connection may be coincidental, it remains noteworthy nonetheless.

Additionally, both figures are associated with keening and lamentation. Brigit appears later in this section as Ireland's original keener. At the same time, the *Cailleach* mourns her lost youth in the anonymous poem *The Lament of the Old Woman of Beare*, where she appears as an aged woman who once enjoyed beauty and the companionship of kings.[6] They both had foster children; Saint Brigid was a foster mother to Christ, and the *Cailleach* had fifty foster children in Beara.[7] The number three connects both goddesses profoundly. Brigit governs the three months of spring and manifests as a triple goddess – either as three sisters all named Brigit, or as three aspects within one deity: healing, poetry and smithcraft. The *Cailleach* mirrors this pattern, representing the three months of winter in Scotland. In Ireland, she forms her own trinity as *Cailleach Bhéarra* alongside her sister hags, *Cailleach* Bolus and *Cailleach Corca Duibne*, who dwelt in Dingle and Iveragh, respectively.[8] Both have strong connections to waters and wells. Both Brigid and the *Cailleach* were revered as divine seers, possessing skills in prophecy. In a translation of *The Lament of the Old Woman of Beare*, it is said that her right eye was taken to buy land that is hers forever.[9]

The one eye features in Brigid's lore, too, where it is said she wishes to make herself ugly to avoid marriage. She loses an eye, rendering herself unattractive to her suitor. Once she is free and takes her veil, she replaces the eye into its socket by herself.[10] The *Cailleach* is said to have red teeth and white hair, signifying the Otherworld.[11] Despite all of these commonalities, the most significant similarity between the *Cailleach* and Brigit is, undoubtedly, that both were Christianised from pagans into nuns.[12]

The *Cailleach* is a pre-Celtic goddess older than time itself.[13] As goddess and queen of winter, she defines longevity. She is the goddess of the ancestors who dwell in the *sídhe*. She represents cold, darkness and death. She is described as having a blue hue to her skin and is generally depicted with one eye, possibly signifying the ability to see into the Otherworld or to denote the gift prophesy.

The *Cailleach* is the supernatural elder and nature-spirit, traditionally viewed as shaping the very topography of the land. Within her landscape, the Otherworld is said to exist. According to folklore, she carries a wand capable of withering autumn vegetation with a single strike. Come spring, tradition holds that she wields this same magic wand in the first week of April, attempting to strike down the new greenery.[14] Like Brigit, the *Cailleach* has travelled and taken on unique identities abroad.

Both Brigit (*Bride* in Scottish Gaelic) and the *Cailleach* maintain powerful traditions in Scotland. The *Cailleach* has a strong connection with water, guarding wells and forming lochs in Scotland.[15] At various places in Scotland, she retained her youth by drinking the water of wells. At the start of each century, on the Hebrides Island of Mull, she renewed her youth by birthing at dawn in a lake before a bird called, a dog barked, or the sun rose.[16]

Among the most prominent *Cailleacha* is the *Cailleach Bhéarra*. The Beara Peninsula in West Cork, Ireland, marks the legendary arrival point of the Milesians, who displaced the mythical Tuatha Dé Danann into the underworld. Beneath the earth, beneath the mounds, they reside, immortal and present in her land. Notably, the south-west of Ireland was historically associated with the Otherworld, particularly that of the dead.[17]

The *Corc Loighdhe* of the Beara Peninsula claimed her as their ancestress. The *Corca Dhuibhne* (neighbour) claimed her as their foster mother. She dropped cairns onto hills in Meath out of her apron, was responsible for moving islands in Kerry, built mountains from rocks carried in her creel in Scotland, and was queen of the Limerick fairies.[18] This death spirit is the primal mother of Ireland, a capable creatrix with supernatural strength, and according to Murphy, linked to the fairies.[19]

Connecting the *Cailleach* and Brigid as opposite aspects of the same spirit reveals how the earliest Irish mother-goddess figure unified contradictory elements: the virginal maiden of new life and the wise crone at the end of life.[20] The early Irish mother-goddess is depicted as both the life-giver and destroyer. This demonstrates how death was associated with every goddess, Brigit included. Yet modern understanding has forgotten this, focusing solely on her light. Denying her deathly components diminishes both her historical significance to devotees and her complete nature today.

Much can be gleaned about deities and their functions from the spellings of their names. The name *Cailleach* literally means witch. Witch is typically linked to older adults who are wizened at this stage of their life's journey. There is also a resemblance between the stem *Cailleach* and the stem in *Cailín*, which means girl in Irish. This arguably reinforces the notion of the same spirit at opposite ends of the continuum. Her name was Boí, meaning older adult or a hag of great age. Boí is synonymous with the word for a cow. Belief in Ireland held that an old cow-goddess lived on an island off the western coast *(Corc Duibne)*. At the tip of the Beara Peninsula is an island called Inis Boi, now called Oileán Baoi, which was/is regarded as her home. The cow is most associated with Brigit, especially in her guise as a

Christianised saint. The *Cailleach* also means 'veiled one.' Like Brigid, she too was made into a nun with the advent of Christianity.[21] Similarly, like Brigid, she is liminal, straddling the pagan and Christian worlds as both a powerful creatrix and a demonised nun. The veil most probably references a nun, but the veil might also signify beyond the veil, as in the Otherworld.

The *Cailleach* is a special manifestation of the land goddess. Brigit, as the consort to King Bres, immediately became a sovereign goddess through her marriage to him. The *Cailleach* is the dark Celtic mother who rules the dark part of the year. During this time of the year, she descends into the Underworld to incubate the seeds of new life. The seeds will emerge through the land at *Imbolc*, conceivably in the personage of Brigit.

Although Celtic divinities were often represented as triads, they also included dual or two-faced goddesses, such as Áine and Grian. The Celts divided the year into two: the dark half and the light half. The two parts of the year were *Geimhreadh* (winter) and *Samhraidh* (summer). The *Cailleach* is a central sovereignty figure said to have a high-pitched cry (similar to the *Bean Sí*). The *Cailleach* could legitimately be considered queen of the dark and Brigit as queen of the light.

Mackenzie's *Wonder Tales from Scottish Myth and*

Legend records a song about the *Cailleach* singing a lamenting song as she wandered about during winter. Within the lyrics, there is evidence to suggest they are two sides of the same coin:

> O life that ebbs like the sea!
> I am weary and old, I am weary and old--
> Oh! How can I be happy
> All alone in the dark and the cold.
>
> I'm the old *Beira* again,
> My mantle no longer is green,
> I think of my beauty with pain
> And the days when another was queen.
>
> My arms are withered and thin,
> My hair, once golden, is grey;
> 'Tis winter--my reign doth begin--
> The youth's summer has faded away.
>
> Youth's summer and autumn have fled--
> I am weary and old, I am tired and old.
> Every flower must fade and fall dead
> When the winds blow cold, when the winds blow cold.

In the song, her lament about returning to old age and her mantle no longer being green becomes apparent. This could be interpreted as a never-ending seesaw of night and day, represented by the *Cailleach* and Brigit, who symbolise life and death.[22]

The Myth of the *Cailleach* and Brigid

A Scottish tale recounts how the winter hag, known as *Cailleach Beira*, captured the summer maiden Bride and held her prisoner in her mountain hall beneath Ben Nevis, Scotland's tallest mountain. Here, she kept her captive and forced her to do menial tasks. The hag captured and restricted the maiden Bride because her son Oenghus had dreamed of her and fallen in love. Angus was an ever-youthful god (characteristic of an Otherworld being). The hag knew that the union of Angus and Bride would mean the end of her reign.

Oenghus lived in Ireland. He turned to the king of Ireland and sought his advice. The king advised Oenghus to wait until the flowers bloomed and the grass turned green before attempting to rescue Bride. But Oenghus could not wait. On his white horse (white horses being symbolic of the Otherworld), he set off to Scotland and searched high and low for Bride.

The hag deterred him repeatedly by raising gales that blew him back to the Emerald Isle. But again and again he returned, determined to find Bride. And see her he did. Eventually, the lovers met, and to mark their joy, the first day of spring became known as Bride's Day. They were found in the fairy forest by a company of fairy ladies who took them to the fairy court to be married.

Beira put up excellent resistance, but youth and vitality were not on her side. In despair, she fled, making her way to the Isle of Skye, where she found rest on the summit of the Old Wife's Ben

(Ben-e-Caillich) at Broadford. She sat gazing across the sea, waiting until day and night would be of equal length. All day, she wept tears of sorrow for her lost power, and when night came, she went to Ireland, where at dawn the next day she drank the magic waters of the Well of Youth and became a young girl. Others claim she turned into a standing stone waiting for the seasons to turn.[23]

The *Cailleach* is notably called upon for protection during wild weather and storms. Moving away from Brigit's possible connection to the *Cailleach*, ample evidence in Brigit's lore in Ireland demonstrates her natural affiliation with death.

Keening

Brigit is heralded as the first keener in Ireland. The story goes that at the death of her son Ruadán, Brigit shrieked at first, cried at last.[24] Ruadán (meaning red-haired) was the son of the goddess Brigit and King Bres. Like Bres, Ruadán was born to parents of two opposing tribes, the Tuatha Dé Danann on his mother's side and the Fomorians on his father's. Despite the union between the goddess and Bres, the Fomorians and the Tuatha Dé Danann were bitter enemies. The Fomorians were giant sea-dwellers and pirates. In contrast to the Tuatha Dé Danann, the Fomorians were associated with death, winter and darkness. When Bres took over, his reign was so miserly that the land dried up in response. The land stopped providing and people were starving. Halls that were once filled with music and storytelling were now silenced. Bres was too mean to pay the bards and poets or invite them to his table in exchange for their services. Musicians, poets and storytellers, once held in the greatest esteem in Irish Celtic society and seated as guests of honour at banquets, were reduced in status, recognition and worth. The land, culture and morale were miserable under the reign of Bres.

Regular fighting ensued between the Tuatha Dé Danann and the Fomorians. Yet, the number of the Tuatha Dé Dannan warriors, in contrast to the Fomorians, stayed the same. No matter how many were killed, the number of warriors on the Tuatha Dé Danann side never dropped. The reason was that the weapons used each day were re-sharpened after battle in the forge by Goibniu, the sacred blacksmith of the Tuatha Dé Danann. As a result, the weapons could harm none. This was an issue for Ruadán.

As was the custom at that time, much respect was given to those, like Goibniu, who were adept at smithcraft. The blacksmiths were held in the highest of esteem in their communities. They were deemed to be of the Otherworld. The very act of transforming the old and fashioning it into something new was regarded as an extraordinary, magical ability that was not of this world.

Ruadán went to Goibniu to ask him to make a spear for him. When the spear was ready and wiped clean, Goibniu handed it to Ruadán. Ruadán quickly took the spear in his hands and threw it at him. It struck Goibniu and he fell to the ground. Although the spear pierced his skin and wounded him, it did not kill him. With astonishing strength, Goibniu pulled the spear out from his body and threw it at Ruadán. The spear pierced Ruadán's heart, killing him instantly.

At that moment, Brigit morphed into a death goddess. The loudest wails and soul-searching moans rang out across the land of Ireland. For the first time, crying and shrieking were heard in Erin. This was the keen. From the depths of despair, Brigit's haunting keen swept across the island of Ireland and down into the Otherworld. The keen of Brigit was in response to the murder of her son. It was in response to her own son's attempt to remove the tribe of the goddess. At the time of her lament, society, culture and spiritual practices were also 'dying'. Brigit's keen was an eerie announcement that a new age was being born, an age where goddess devotion and worship would cease to be. It was a cry for the pain of the mothers of Ireland that would be seen, heard and felt at the hands of patriarchy. It was a stark warning that for Bres, there was no going back. His rule had facilitated

Ruadán's actions and his time as sovereign ruler was over.

As Brigit is claimed to be the original keener in Ireland, there is an apparent connection between her and death. Keening is viewed as a national form of poetic expression. It was a tradition that existed in Ireland until the Catholic church eradicated it in the 1950s. Keening women served as a kind of 'psychopomp who presides over the transition in which the whole community finds itself'.[25] The keening tradition became known as 'keening their dead'. Older women of the neighbourhood would come into the wake house crying over the corpse and reciting praises of the deceased. Together, they came to mourn and wail the loss of one of their own and encourage the rest of the community to release their sorrow collectively. As sombre and mournful as this tradition was, there was also another side of keening that contained an element of mischief. Between death and burial keening, women had a *carte blanche* to ridicule and call out politics, the clergy and even the deceased. They often did this in Irish so nobody would understand. This can be interpreted, for those unable to understand the lyrics, as almost speaking in riddles, or in a tongue from the Otherworld. There would undoubtedly have been fun to be had amidst the theatrics of their performance, voicing gossip, secrets and openly ridiculing people, either alive or dead, at the most inappropriate time. This same powerful ability with words was used by the keening women. Power through words is connected to Brigit in her guise as goddess of poetry.

Psychopomp

Individual Christian clergypersons were said to have considered fairies as beings who lacked human souls, yet could escort the souls of the faithfully departed to the gates of heaven.[26]

This can be seen as further evidence of a typical negating attitude toward pre-Christian customs and the demotion of once-venerated gods and goddesses into fairies.

Brigit is not generally acknowledged as a psychopomp, but references to her in this role exist. A psychopomp is a figure who acts as a bridge to help the departed soul cross over into eternal life. The psychopomp is a guardian, a conductor of souls back to the Otherworld. For such a role to exist, a belief in the continuation of life beyond the physical is required. This would certainly apply to the religious beliefs, practices and customs of the Irish Celtic people.

Brigit played the role of psychopomp through the keen.[27] Keening was a process that enabled the departed soul to leave the physical body. The keen instigated the soul's departure and this began with Brigit. The role of the psychopomp, therefore, came from the keen. The psychopomp held space or contained the soul whilst it made its transition from the physical body back to the collective. Brigit, as psychopomp, is not alone in this role in Irish Celtic mythology. The Morrigan, as a death goddess who foretells the outcomes of battles and predicts death, also serves as a psychopomp. It is sometimes understood that the Morrigan, because of her relationship to the Dagda, is one of Brigit's presumed mothers.[28] If this is accepted, then perhaps the ability to psychopomp could have been passed down from mother to daughter.

The connection between the keen, the role of psychopomp and Brigit reveals the centrality and power of the voice in these roles. The voice was an essential tool for the Irish Celts. The oral tradition was the primary method for recording stories, poetry and healing practices in Irish Celtic society. Brigit, as the goddess of poets and poetry, was venerated for her skill in communication and her ability to impart poetic *Imbas*. People venerated and sought help from Brigit for all matters related to oratory. Even today, Brigit is said to be the muse of choice for many writers, journalists, singers and all those who work with the voice.

Brigit has been honoured for her exceptional communication abilities, which bring light to inspiration and clarity through her voice. Yet her ability to give voice to sorrow and pain, or to use voice to hold space for grief, remains largely unacknowledged. The light and dark aspects of human life are present in all goddesses. Their skill sets apply to both the lighter and darker issues faced by humanity. If Brigit can be called upon to give voice to words that bring joy and lightness to the world, she can equally be called upon to give voice to grief and sorrow in the face of death.

Brigit is said to have invented the whistle for signalling at night.[29] This was likely for the protection of women. The invention of the whistle for signalling at night is also related to Brigid's role as a Psychopomp. In Irish superstition, according to Kelly, whistling is associated with ill fortune and with the Otherworld.[30]

In Irish mythology, the king assumed true sovereignty by uniting with one of the goddesses of the land. The goddess typically transformed once the union had taken place.[31] After King Bres unites with the Goddess Brigit, she begins her transformation, which is completed with the death of their only son Ruadán. With his death, Brigit transforms into arguably the original *Bean Chaointe*.

The Banshee

The Banshee is often referred to as the *Bean Sí* or *Bean Chaointe*. *Bean Chaointe* literally translates to 'keening woman' or 'crying woman'. Brigit may connect to the *Bean Chaointe* for several reasons. Firstly, Brigit invented the keen. The keen is one of the most prominent traits associated with the female supernatural death-messenger in Irish traditions. By all accounts, she wails loudly for the family member who is soon to die. The *Bean Sí* is said to be a woman of the fairy hills/Otherworld.[32]

From the National Folklore Collection, we are told that the *Bean Sí* is generally 'a small wee woman' dressed in white.[33] Brigit is more often than not depicted as a virginal maiden, clad in white. One account from the folklore collection describes the *Bean Sí* as wearing a red skirt and without feet.[34] While there has never been an account of Brigit without feet, the reference to red, through the lens of the Otherworld and Brigit, bears noting. The *Bean Sí* is often described as combing her long, red hair, which parallels that of Brigit. In other accounts, her hair is described as golden, but it is also reported to be red in Armagh, Roscommon and Westmeath. From the National Folklore Collection, we read of the prominence of the number three with the *Bean Sí*. The *Bean Sí* is said to tap the window three times or knock the door three times before a person dies.[35] One account tells us that three coughs were often heard as a person was dying.[36] In almost all transcripts, the wail of the *Bean Sí* is heard three times. The number three featured in these accounts arguably suggests a connection to Brigit, given her typical association with this number. The *Bean Sí* generally concentrates her attention on the most important family members, in particular, the oldest male member. This also applies to Brigit, as well as Ruadán. In the case of Rúadán, though, he is the *only* male member. *Bean Sí* literally means 'woman of the *sí*', a fairy woman, or a woman of the mounds/hills. There can be no doubt that the *Bean Sí*, 'fairy woman', and *Bean Sí*, supernatural female death-messenger, are the same expression.[37] Accepting this connection suggests that Brigit could feasibly have played the role of *Bean Sí*.

The *Bean Sí* is a solitary figure. A solitary crying female supernatural being who is perceived as an ancestress of the family she attends. She is an omen or messenger of death, not its cause. The *Bean Sí* is described as beautiful, wearing a long grey cloak over a green dress, with her eyes deep red from crying.[38] Others say she wears white with red shoes.[39] She is said to be dressed in red, white, or grey. Red is associated with fairies as well as with magic and the supernatural. White is another dominant colour for her, and notably, Brigid's nuns were originally dressed in white. The *Bean Sí* is sometimes seen wearing a cloak or mantle, similar to Brigid's traditional garment.

The *Bean Sí* is not only connected to death, but death is her most prominent trait. This echoes how each goddess embodies birth, death and rebirth, which ebb and flow into moments of dominance and subjugation. The *Bean Sí* is noticed mainly when someone is about to die or has just died, as with Brigit and Ruadán. Her appearance is also politically based. Her appearance serves as a foreboding about people whose actions and deaths will have a decisive bearing on the future political and economic well-being of the region.[40]

This description is essential. Brigit's keen was for her son Ruadán, but also as a warning to Bres, the king and her husband and to the people of Ireland, that his miserly reign was coming to an end. It was also a lament for the way of the great goddess. Her time of veneration and respect was over. Her keen was for all the men who would perish in battle. Her wail was for all the mothers of Ireland, herself included. Times, they were a-changing and not for the better.

The *Bean Sí* can sound like nocturnal animals. Among many animals, she has been reported to sound like the Screachán Ríoghach.[41] The screech owl is the animal most associated with Maman

Brigitte, the death goddess/lwa. Its piercing shriek in the dead of the night is to alert either danger about to befall or to announce the transitioning of a soul from this world to the next.

There are many accounts of hearing the *Bean Sí* wail three times. Three is a magical, supernatural number in Ireland and is very much connected to the goddess. The *Bean Sí* is said to follow the bereaved family. Her wail encircles the house and follows the course of the stream or the river. She is said to sometimes be beautiful and at other times considered a hag (reminiscent of Brigit and the *Cailleach*). She has long hair, similar to the professional keeners who also had long hair. Long flowing hair is also characteristic of a supernatural or Otherworld woman.[42]

Even with a death abroad, she has been heard at the exact time of the passing in Ireland. In one record from Westmeath, she carried her tidings from the West Indies to Ireland. The West Indies is a significant place, as it reflects Maman Brigitte, who originated in the West Indies. The *Bean Sí* has been reported to appear near water sources, such as lakes, rivers, or wells. She has also been known to appear at the border-hours: dawn, midnight or dusk – her favoured times. These hours belong to the Otherworld. These times are also associated with the birth of Saint Brigid. She was said to have been born neither on a day nor on a night, neither inside nor outside.

The *Bean Sí* is known as 'the Bow' (pronounced *Bo*, Irish for cow) in Wexford. Staying in Wexford, the Banshee is explicitly linked to Bride Street and Black Cow Lane. The *Bean Sí* is also said to be heard in the chair-shaped rocks. This resembles the Hag's chair at Slieve na Cailleach, connecting back to the possible link between Brigit and the *Cailleach*.

The *Bean Sí*, however, unlike Brigid, is reported to be feisty. She can be aggressive when she comes looking for what is hers, such as when her comb is lost. The inappropriate touching of women or speaking unkindly to women makes her react by lashing out and leaving the imprint of her five fingers. Although it is never claimed that Brigit, as a goddess or Brigid the saint, is aggressive, the loyalty and dedication to the safety of women is common to both the pagan deity and the Christian saint.

War and combat are direct passageways to death and entry into the Otherworld. As Saint Brigid, she was reportedly vehemently opposed to all warfare and combat. Yet Kelly identifies her as the sovereign goddess of Leinster, as well as the goddess of war and death. Brigit served as the tutelary goddess of Leinster.[43] She was the patroness of Leinstermen and thought to favour them in times of war.[44]

Weber tells us that Celtic deities were literal representations of forces of nature, which could be unpredictable and not always benevolent.[45] Goddesses were feared much more than beloved. In the *Annals of Tigernach*, the battle of Luachair gained by Cairbre over the Uí Néill, the following was said:

> The fierce battle of Luachair above, downwards
> Brigit was seen, no empty vision
> Noble was the bloody battle of Findabair
> Round Illada's body after death.[46]

In the *Vita Prima*, Brigit is described as going into battle when Ulster invaded Leinster in the Battle of Allen in 718 or 722, 'with her staff in her right hand and a column of fire blazing skywards from her head'.[47]

It is said that the sight of their sovereign goddess willing them on to stand their ground and protect what was theirs encouraged the Leinster army.

Stokes describes Brigit's appearance to the Leinstermen in *The Battle of Allen*, based on the version of the text in the *Yellow Book of Lecan*, as follows:

> Now in that battle, the mind of Columkill did not rest
>   or stay for the Húi Néill,
> For above the battalion of Leinster, he saw Brigit,
> terrifying the host of Conn's Half,
> whereupon, seeing Brigit in that wise,
> Aed, the king of South Leinster, routed Fergal and the
>   Northerners.[48]

These descriptions suggest that, although she may not have incited battle, she was no pushover. When her territory and her people came under attack, she appeared – willing them on to defend what was theirs.

Although medieval texts never *explicitly* crown her a fairy queen, the absence of a named queen for Leinster invites that Brigit could reasonably be considered a fairy queen of Leinster.

Well-known fairy queens also functioned as *Bean Sí*, appearing to keen when members of their connected families died. Perhaps Brigit – as Ireland's original keener – did not keen for just one family but regarded the entire Irish race as her kin, positioning herself as matron of the country. Though her territory began in Leinster, her influence spread across the island and beyond, much like her goddess lore. The Irish people – her *Tuatha* – became her extended family, making it plausible to identify Brigit as a *Bean Sí*.

4

BRIGIT'S OTHERWORLDLY ABILITIES

'Those (fairies) in the Irish stories are fairly clearly former pagan deities, reimagined as aristocratic superhumans inhabiting a parallel world located within hills or ancient burial mounds or on islands.'[1]

These former pagan deities mentioned by Hutton very much include Brigit for various reasons, such as: hills are synonymous with the literal meaning of her name, and brig is 'most high'. Ancient burial mounds at Newgrange, Meath and others created by her father, the Dagda, were/are places where she guided souls home to the Otherworld in her position as psychopomp. Islands mentioned by Hutton are most certainly inclusive of the Emerald Island itself, Ireland, of which she is the sovereign goddess. If the essence of Brigit has manifested in many guises, shapes and forms, as goddess and saint in Ireland, as Brigantia in England and Maman Brigitte in the Caribbean, then she could be considered in an elemental form as a nature spirit venerated in the old Irish religion on this land.

Within Cogitosus' *Lives of Brigid*,[2] the *Vita Prima*[3] and the *Bethu Brigte*,[4] common themes run through the lives and stories that arguably depict a supernatural, otherworldly image. Throughout these documented lives, the stories describe a charitable, virginal saint who has the ability to create abundance, perform miraculous healing and offer protection to women and to the vulnerable. These miracles appear steeped in supernatural magic such as wish granting, creating abundance, manifestation, healing and even cursing.

The chief concern of the fairy folk is the natural world and all its inhabitants, especially animals. Interwoven in many of her stories is also the frequent mention of animals, which further reflects her elemental nature. When speaking of Brigid, Cogitosus says that 'The whole of nature, beasts, cattle and birds, was subjected to her power'.[5]

Saint Brigid's miracles are all told through the lens of Christianity. What was once magic and the goddess became miracles and the saint. It is God who is credited with the wonders he performs through Brigid. However, nothing is as it seems at first glance. Most accounts of Saint Brigid were written from a biased perspective. Indeed, her veneration arose and evolved as Christianity gradually superseded paganism. The recorded *Lives of Brigid* do not acknowledge her as a goddess. Suppose these accounts omitted this former 'face' of Brigit. In that case, it is likely that the even older aspect of her known within the old Irish religion – the fairy faith of Ireland – was also deliberately left out.

There will always be uncertainty surrounding the Otherworld and the fairies. Whether they exist at all remains open to question. No one can fully define who or what they are, or even confirm that they are. Despite centuries of speculation and study, knowledge of them remains elusive – a hazy space where imagination and belief intertwine. The Otherworld, in this sense, is less a place to be proven than an idea to be sensed.

When describing fairies and their abilities, beings capable of shapeshifting and assuming new identities at will often come to mind. Not all inhabitants of the Otherworld share this gift, yet it seems an ordinary skill among them. This same quality appears in Brigit. No other spirit displays such an uncanny capacity as she does. It is most evident when we consider Brigit as a goddess who evolved into a Christian saint – 'Brigid was part of the old Irish religion that continued into the Christian culture.'[6]

If Saint Brigid is understood as a euhemerised pagan goddess, it may be possible to look further back and consider her connection to the Old Irish religion, the fairy faith of Ireland, as another aspect of her many guises. Within this framework, Brigid can also be viewed as a fairy woman, a lady of the Irish Otherworld.

Despite ongoing debate over whether she should be regarded as a goddess or a saint, the qualities most admired in her clearly overlap. In Celtic society, her primary role as a pagan goddess was to ensure fertility and safeguard the well-being of the land, particularly its animals and crops.[7]

These traits would also come to define her new identity as a Christian saint. However, whether approached from whatever angle, she is venerated; there is a shared ground where her devotees meet, drawn to her for the same essential reasons. Interpretations may differ, but at her core, she is recognised and honoured for the same enduring qualities, regardless of the title she bears.

Among the most cherished aspects of Brigid are her concern for women, her protection of them and her role in establishing sisterhoods – first as circles of priestesses and later as convents of nuns. Equally valued are her charity, generosity, maternal nature and advocacy for those on the margins of society. Both goddess and saint, Brigid carries within her a spark of humour, mischief and enchantment – qualities that make her spirit both relatable and intensely beloved.

What follows presents, in alphabetical order, many of her magical abilities as recorded in the *Lives of Brigid*, the *Vita Prima* and the *Bethu Brigte*. These uncanny gifts, infused with the energy of the Otherworld, illuminate the fairy face of Brigit.

Powers such as the creation of abundance and the act of manifestation reveal areas where her aid may still be sought. The animals, elements, colours and other symbols woven throughout her stories each hold a magical resonance, serving as conduits for connection with this enduring, otherworldly aspect of Brigit.

Abundance

Brigid created abundance when the cupboards were bare, either in her own house or in the homes of others. This was mostly done to cover her tracks, to trick, as it were, her superiors or guests after she had given food or items to people experiencing poverty. In the first story mentioned by Cogitosus, she is sent by her mother, an enslaved person, to churn butter. Brigid does as she is instructed, but gives it all away to people in need. When it comes to her time to hand in her day's work, the butter is miraculously restored.[8]

The Vita Prima of St Brigid, 11.8 (ed. Connolly), records that any food Brigid's hand touched or her eye saw was instantly multiplied. In 14.2, when preparing food for guests, Brigid gives piece after piece of meat to a begging dog. Starting with only five pieces, she has little to begin with. An amazed guest watches this happen and is further shocked when, at serving time, the meat has miraculously been restored.

In 99.1, when the bishops came to visit and she

had no food to give them, she milked the same cow three times and produced enough milk from the one cow that would typically have come from three. In 28.4, she blesses water and turns it into beer. In the twenty-sixth story, Cogitosus writes of a weary Brigid arriving at a woman's house, having travelled all day. The woman has no fire or food. She puts her loom into the fire and slays the cow's calf to cook over it. The next morning, the calf had been replaced with another, as well as the loom. Cogitosus also tells us in the twenty-ninth story that a poor man approaches her looking for honey. Again, she has none. But she hears, beneath the floors, the humming of bees. When the floor was dug up and explored, there was enough honey to satisfy the man.[9]

Animals

Many of Brigid's stories, as mentioned in the *Life of Saint Brigid*, the *Vita Prima* and the *Bethu Brigte*, include animals such as cows, dogs, sheep, cattle, horses, wild boar, pigs, wolves, foxes, ducks and bees. The frequent inclusion of animals in these stories reflects her otherworldly connections and her protective nature over all beings, including animals. As a goddess, Brigit is the guardian of domestic animals, surrounded by two oxen, Fea and Feimhean, and Triath, king of the swine. The goddess has a similar role to Saint Brigid, who, in folk culture, is the patroness of farm animals and crops. The Feast Day of Brigit is *Imbolg*, which directly references the birth of young animals in spring.[10]

In the *Vita Prima*, 27.1, a stubborn cow would not budge without her missing calf, but yet moves for Brigid, and as a consequence, the missing calf suddenly reappears. In 50.3, a horse breaks free from the chariot that contains Brigid, but she remains unharmed. In 107.1, we read a story of how Brigid can tame wild animals. The story goes that a wild boar joined her herd of swine. Upon blessing it, it calmed down and settled into the herd. In 124, she calls ducks to join her from the water.

Colours red and green

Brigit is closely associated with the colours red, white and green. As an Irish goddess, she embodies the spirit of the Emerald Isle and is often depicted wearing either green or white. White, the colour worn by Ireland's earliest nuns, evokes purity and devotion. As a goddess, she is often depicted with vivid red hair, a hue traditionally associated with combat and vitality. Though not a war goddess, Brigit's role as patron of smithcraft connected her to the making and distribution of weapons in times of conflict. Red, in its purest sense, signifies blood and life force, qualities that align with the life-giving nature of the mother goddess.

When shifting attention to the Irish Otherworld, these colours also feature there. Red is the colour of the Otherworld and a colour that is often associated with solitary fairies such as the *Bean Sí*.[11]

It is also a colour considered magical, as it was believed to resist the power of evil spirits.[12]

The merfolk wear red hats with feathers and can shapeshift into either hornless cows or human females with green hair. The leprechaun typically appears as an old man dressed in green, though sometimes in red. The *Fear Dearg* (The Red Man) is a figure of combat. The *Púca* is usually greenish-black but can also appear white. The *Cú Sidhe*, the fairy dog, is generally dark black-green, though sometimes white with one or two red ears. This combination of red and white echoes the cow that features prominently in many Christian depictions of Brigid.

Cows

There is an understanding that some cattle breeds originated with the fairies. The 'Mollie' or 'Moyline' is a breed of cattle that goes back in time to the Irish Iron Age.[13]

Several historians suggest that the Morrígan may have been Brigit's mother. In early tradition, the Morrígan is said to have owned a herd of white cows with red ears, animals long associated with the Otherworld. Though best known as a goddess of war, she also possessed powers of shapeshifting and prophecy – qualities that mark her as a being of the liminal realms. Cattle and cows likewise appear throughout Brigit's miracles and in many of the early, pre-tenth-century *Lives*, continuing the symbolic connection between both goddesses and the sacred herds of the Otherworld.[14] The Morrígan is sometimes identified as Badb, or as part of a triad that includes Badb, a name also used for the *Bean Sí*, the fairy woman whose keening heralds death.[15] Another figure sometimes identified as Brigit's mother is Boann, the goddess of the River Boyne. This connection is plausible given her union with the Dagda and the birth of their son, Oenghus. Ptolemy's *Geography* of the second century records that the earlier name of the River Boyne was *Bouvinda*, meaning 'white cow'. Both of Brigit's potential mothers share associations with cattle.[16]

The Celts likely had an ancient tradition of regarding white cattle as having a special connection to the Otherworld.[17] White red-eared cows are also linked to the deities of the Otherworld.[18] This connects Brigit and the Otherworld once more. In the *Vita Prima*, in 11.7, we read that Brigid, as a young child, was reared on the milk of an otherworldly cow. Interestingly, cattle can also be associated with mourning and lamenting. Cattle are said to lament their dead herd and cast their horns in token of their sorrow. The milk of the sacred cow was one of the earliest sacred foods throughout the world. Milk from the holy cow was believed to provide an antidote to the poison of weapons. The sacred cow symbolised the sanctity of motherhood. Through her milk, life was nourished and sustained.[19] This otherworldly animal sometimes emerges from caves that appear suddenly, or by coming ashore from the sea, lakes or rivers. These natural places were traditionally regarded as access points to the Otherworld. Kelly tells us that the cow is an animal of the Otherworld.[20] The enchanted cow uses caves and bodies of water to emerge from and return to the Otherworld. The cow sometimes has a female companion who may be a mermaid or a woman with special associations with water. The female is an emissary from the Otherworld.[21] A tale from Inisbofin (island of the white cow) tells of a fisherman and his son spotting a beautiful lady dressed in green driving a white cow into a lake.

The mythical cow was once associated with the cult of Goibniu, smithy extraordinaire of the Tuatha Dé Danann. The enchanted cow carries *Bean Sí* associations. Kelly tells us that the island of Inchbofin is so called because of the White Cow that appears on the lake before somebody is about to drown in the lake or perish in a storm.[22]

Even though white and red-eared cows were said to be of the Otherworld, they did, in fact, exist in

Ireland.[23] Eighteen herds of white red-eared cows could be seen roaming the Irish countryside. Similar breeds were also found in Britain. The imagery of goddesses in Irish lore derives from a complex of beliefs once current among the Celts overseas.[24]

Cattle played a central role in Ireland's economy for thousands of years. Cows provided milk, butter, cheese and leather, while oxen were used for ploughing, hauling wagons and supplying bones and horns for sewing tools. Possession of cattle was a primary indicator of wealth and social status.

There is no specific cow goddess in Celtic literature, although several Irish goddesses, such as Bóann and The Morrigan, possessed supernatural cows. Brigit possessed her own supernatural cow. Her cow accompanied her or her spirit as she travelled and blessed homes on the eve of her Feast Day. Indeed, many customs on Brigid's day were explicitly designed to protect and bless cattle. Brigid is also associated with the curing of many bovine diseases. At the same time, dairy products form an essential part of the special meal prepared to celebrate her special Day or its Eve.[25] In Christian art, she often appears alongside a white cow with red ears, believed to be from the Otherworld, whose milk is said never to run dry.

The Goddess culture may have Indo-European origins.[26] The ancient Sanskrit collection of hymns, the *Rig Veda*, repeatedly uses the cow as a metaphor for the river-goddess, with the streams of the river being synonymous with the milk flowing from her in her shape as an otherworldly cow.[27] Water from the river made the countryside productive.

The *Druimin Donn Dílis*, The Faithful Brown Whitebacked Cow, is a poetic name for Ireland. According to Irish place-name legend, three cows once emerged from the sea: *Bó Finn* (White cow), *Bó Dub* (Black cow) and *Bó Derg* (Red cow). They set off across the country. The black cow went north, the red cow went south and the white cow went straight across the country.

Drawing parallels to Brigit and the *Cailleach* reveals how the cow features in both. A story of *Corc Duibhne* tells how a mystical woman rears him and a druid called Boí on her island. Each morning, she bathes him in the sea on the back of a white red-eared cow.

In addition to white cows, tales of the white bull also exist. As Ó hÓgáin says, these animals and colours reflect both prosperity and benign otherworldly forces.[28]

'A white bull was killed and one man consumed his fill of its meat and of its soup, and he slept after that meal, and four druids over him sang a charm of truth, and it would be revealed to him then, in a vision the identity of the man to be made king, as to his form and his appearance and the nature of his actions he would do. This was the *tarbhfheis*. The large size of bulls may reflect their supernatural status – a creature of great power, fertility and invincibility, also good fortune.'[29]

Even without a specific cow goddess in Celtic culture, the cow is a global symbol of the goddess. The fact that the Christianised saint is always accompanied by an otherworldly cow can be seen to depict the presence of the nature spirit and the goddess within the saint, which contributed to the miraculous abilities possessed by the saint.

Cursing

Irish fairies are known for their entertaining and mischievous nature.[30] Similarly, as documented in the *Vita Prima*, Brigid's stories possessed a fun quality and she was by no means a pushover. She was 'adept at giving their comeuppance to the arrogant, the undeserving, or those who crossed her'.[31]

Several stories in the *Vita Prima* demonstrate this ability to curse. In 39.6, when a woman insists on telling lies about the paternity of her son, Brigid causes her tongue to swell. In 56.2, a leper asks Brigid to wash his clothes, which she does. She asks a nun to clothe the man while he waits for his clothes to dry. The woman refuses and is consequently 'stricken with exceedingly revolting foulness and leprosy' for the space of an hour. In chapter 74.1, a maidservant flees to Brigid from her mistress. When the mistress tries to grab the maidservant back, her hand becomes withered. In 76.1, two lepers ask Brigid to heal them. One washes the other and is healed. The healed leper refuses to return the favour and is stricken once again with leprosy. In chapter 78.1, a beggar receives a cow from Brigid but shows ingratitude. Brigid forewarns him that the cow will bring him no fortune. In chapter 80.4, Brigid and a charioteer approach a man fencing his field and ask permission to cross through. He refuses. The charioteer pushes past anyway. The man reacts violently, hitting the horses, who kick so hard that Brigid and the charioteer fall off. The man tries to make light of his actions, but collapses and dies. In chapter 87.5, when a man grabs one of Brigid's virgins, his hand goes rigid until he releases her.

Fire

Fire is the most magical of elements. Its destructive yet transformative properties are impressive if not intimidating. Fire is the element most associated with Brigit and features prominently in many of Brigid's stories.

In the *Vita Prima*, chapter 2.4, the bondmaid Broicseach was told by a druid that 'you will give birth to an illustrious daughter who will shine in the world like the sun in the vault of heaven'. Before

Brigid was even born, her light, radiance and fire were prophesied. Many stories of fire surround Brigid, even as an infant. In chapter 7.2, her mother left her one day to go milk cows far from the house. From a distance, the house where infant Brigid lay sleeping appeared to be on fire. In chapter 10, a druid saw a column of fire rising from the little house where she slept. In chapter 8, the druid and bondmaid were sitting when a piece of cloth touched the infant Brigid's head. To their astonishment, the child's head was aglow with fiery flame. When they felt the fabric, the flame disappeared. In chapter 20.2, upon receiving her veil from Bishop Mel, a column of fire appeared rising from Brigid's head to the very top of the church.

Fire was so sacred that her nuns, as reported by Gerald of Wales, 'so carefully and diligently cherish and nurse the fire'. The fire was 'surrounded by a circular hedge of willow within which no male enters'. 'Only women are allowed to blow the fire, and then not with the breath of their mouth but only with bellows or winnowing forks.'[32]

The tradition of fire guardianship belonged exclusively to women, first her priestesses, then her nuns, highlighting both the sacred nature of fire and the sanctity of its protection by her sisterhood.

In Irish homes, Brigid was invoked for protection from fire at night. Prayers said over the fire while covering it with ashes were known as smooring. The word smooring, as described by Alexander Carmichael, is a Scottish word meaning smothering or subduing. The fire was rarely completely extinguished in houses. The fire weakened and the embers lay smouldering as the house slept, only to be rekindled the following morning from the old ashes. No spirit better than Brigit to be associated with fire, given her ability to dwell in liminal space and bridge the old to the new, yesterday to today. The fire was generally in the centre of the home for cooking, heat and socialising. The oldest member of the house slept closest to the fire. Prayers and blessings were said into the hearth as ashes were placed over the flames to suffocate them. Brigid's dual role as both general protectress and protectress from fire is notable. Also noteworthy in the following smooring invocation is the mention of Brigid as being in the middle, which could be interpreted as her liminal, intermediary position between the visible and invisible worlds:

> ***Coigilt na Tine***
>
> *Coiglím an tine seo mar a choiglíonn cách*
> *Críost í mullach an tí is Bríd ina lár*
> *An dá aingeal déag is treise ígcathair na ngrást*
> *Ag cumhdach an tí is na tine seo*
> *Is a mhuintir a thabhairt slán*

Coigilt na Tine

I rake this fire as all do
Christ at the top of the house, and Bridget in its midst
The twelve strongest angels in the city of graces
Keeping this house and this fire
And it's people safe.
(Ceathrú Thaidhg – North Mayo)[33]

On the Scottish and Hebridean islands, Brigid is also connected with the hearth of the home. As in Ireland, the fire was traditionally situated in the centre of the home for cooking, heat and socialising. According to folklore, fire is said to repel fairies. Though the reason remains unclear, tradition holds that fire keeps fairies at bay.

This seems contradictory for Brigit, the lady of the flame and smith. Perhaps the hearth served as a central portal for the fairy folk, and people sought protection from them. If so, Brigit, who inhabits both worlds, serves as the common link between them and can therefore placate all beings while keeping the most malevolent at bay.

Brigit is also the patron deity of metalworkers, who use fire. As a goddess, one of her main domains is smithcraft, forging the new from the old. She creates the latest in this process while dwelling in the liminal space where two worlds merge. In this capacity, she bridges the seemingly incompatible elements of fire and water, yet both are necessary for the desired result. Again, she appears as an intermediary between old and new through smithcraft. In Cormac's glossary, Bishop Cormac Mac Cuillenáin describes Brigid as a woman of smith-work, a *ban goibneachtae*. From this word likely comes Goibniu, listed as one of the leading artisans of the Tuatha Dé Danann. Goibniu was the smith of the divine family, Brigit's family. The skill of smithcraft is considered otherworldly: 'the sight of a man who can yield a stream of brilliant liquid metal from the firing of a certain rough rock evokes a practical wizardry.[34]

The forge where smithcraft took place was traditionally a meeting place for the community. Here, people gathered to chat, gossip and conduct business. Here, they also shared stories of the fairies. The smith served as a bridge for the entire community, creating tools for humans, animals and machinery alike. He was responsible for both weapons of war and everyday implements. The smith was considered noble, a man of high standing who earned a seat at the king's table during feasts.[35] The community credited the smith with otherworldly, magical abilities. Women who could not churn their milk into butter would turn to the blacksmith for help. He would place three red-hot irons on the anvil and butter would immediately appear. He could banish rats and served as a veterinarian for horses, cattle and dogs.[36]

He could heal pain and cure ailments. Even the water that cooled the irons was believed to serve as a cure for warts and other skin issues. People both respected and feared him. With the turn of the anvil, he could curse as easily as cure. The blacksmith also wielded power against fairies, spirits and those who practised evil magic. The most common account of fairies and blacksmiths involved the shoeing of fairy horses. One blacksmith near Tulsk, Roscommon, had standing instructions to be ready on Halloween night to shoe the little travellers' horses for the horse fair.[37]

Healing

Healing was one of Brigit's principal functions as a goddess. Healing, or leechcraft as it was sometimes called, encompassed genius, innovation, herbal knowledge, justice, and words in various forms, poetic verse, incantations, spells, and prayer. In pre-Christian Ireland, society made little provision for the poor, sick and elderly. Those afflicted by poverty, illness, or age-related conditions were often put to death as a solution, since society viewed illness as a curse inflicted by supernatural powers.[38]

Under the Brehon laws, treatment for all patients, regardless of social standing, was enforced by law. Treatment included medicine, attendance allowance and nourishment. Medicine books were passed down through physicians' families, documenting the symptoms of diseases and their corresponding remedies. All remedies were homegrown and sourced locally. Both curative herbs and deadly poisons were known. Healing charms were used either to promote fertility and good luck or to cause death and disease.[39] Pliny reports in his work that the medico-magical practices of the druids were the fundamental basis of their power and influence. While science played a role, equally important were the natural laws and Earth wisdom associated with the mother goddess concept, as well as the role of women practitioners.[40]

Keening also contains healing properties. Brigit, as the original keener and a powerful healer, embodied both mourning and healing.

Fairies are also healers. In the National Folklore Collection, we read:

> The Dananns with their knowledge of arts and crafts and their greatest skill in medicine and the art of healing had always a great pride of race and from their 'high places' looked down literally and figuratively on both the Firbolgs and the Milesians. Still they bore no enmity towards either and never failed when opportunity offered or when requested to use their skill and knowledge of service of their former enemies. This, and many other estimable traits in their character earned for them the title of the 'good people', and when at some later period they voluntarily retired or were forced into invisibility, and became the fairies.[41]

It is noted that all herbs gathered on May Eve, the time of the fairies, are supposed to be endowed with healing power.[42]

Belief in the old ways of appealing to gods and goddesses for their magical healing abilities was replaced by the miracles that became associated with the saints. This was no different with Brigit/Brigid. The saint continued the healing legacy of the goddess. Exceptional individuals, especially those with powers of healing, were said to be 'in the fairies'.[43]

Women healers in Ireland were called *bean feasa*. The west of Ireland was once home to Biddy Early, the most famous healer woman of her time. A bean feasa living in Feakle, Clare, Biddy attracted many visitors seeking her gifts. Her supernatural abilities were so renowned that it was claimed she was 'in the fairies'.

Eddie Lenihan documents stories of Biddy Early's practices: she might refuse to work her magic if insulted or disrespected; she could cure 'infestation' or 'manifestation by fairies'; and her powers came with conditions, never accepting money but only offerings. The bottle typically associated with Biddy was said to have been given to her by either her deceased son or deceased brother, depending on the storyteller. Was Biddy working on behalf of the dead, or was she one of them? Her ability to see and communicate with the dead, combined with her power to appease the fairies, suggests an innate connection to the Otherworld.

On Brigit's own turf, in Leinster, another great *bean feasa* lived by the name of Moll Anthony. Moll

Anthony was considered a witch and lived at the Red Hills beside the Hill of Allen. 'People went to Moll for cures for persons & animals'.⁴⁴ It is said that she passed on the cures to her sons before her death. Sometimes, to cure the cattle, she would make up two bottles of medicine, and one of these had to be broken, while the other was given to the sick animals. People came from all parts of Ireland to her. In addition to Biddy Early in Clare and Moll Anthony of the Red Hills, Nan O'Toole of Galway and Maurice Griffin in Kerry were all renowned healers in Ireland who, it seems, all got their abilities from the fairies.⁴⁵

In *The Life of Saint Brigid* by Cogitosus, many stories document Saint Brigid's nationwide miracles. These miracles include causing a lying woman's tongue to swell, restoring sight to a blind man, giving speech to a mute girl, restoring a worker's missing hand and curing a leper. Another story tells how Brigid healed the king, who had two horses' ears in place of human ears. The story goes that after she had shaved the king's head, he felt two human ears where the horses' ears had been.⁴⁶

Immortality

Fairy kings and queens were said to be endowed with Immortality. Brigit herself, moving from a pre-Christian goddess to a Christian saint to a Vodou lwa, Maman Brigitte and possibly from

Brigantia, is suggestive of her immortality, akin to fairy kings and queens.

Land

The Laighean people gave their name to the kingdom of Leinster, of which Brigit was the tutelary goddess, and as such, she was as much concerned with its political as with its economic well-being. As protectress of the land, she shares this trait with the Otherworld beings, who protect their realm from humans unless they explicitly invite them in.[47] The Laighean people shared territory with the Fothairt tribe, who also held territory in Offaly near Croghan Hill, where some believe that Saint Brigid was born. There is another, more widely held view that Brigid, as the historical saint, was born in Faughart, Louth.

'In times of war, Saint Brigid was wont to make herself visible to intervene in favour of the Leinstermen and more or less in the manner of the pagan war-goddess.'[48]

Rivers throughout Ireland bear female names. They carry the names of Otherworld women, such as *Bóinn* for the River Boyne and *Sionann* for the River Shannon. A variation of Brigid's name, *Bride*, is also the name of a river that runs through Cork and Waterford. In the United Kingdom, rivers are similarly named after Brigid: the River Braint in Wales and the River Brent in England. Brigit is closely connected to the land, both as a goddess and an elemental being.

Fairies and elemental spirits are inherently part of nature herself. They are concerned with the land, acting as its sovereign protectors, and with all its inhabitants and sentient beings. Trees, crystals, mountains, rocks and forests all house spirits that dwell within them, acting not only as protectors of these spaces but also as healers to humans who are still enough to feel their guidance. Within nature, the essence of the goddess and the spirit of the Otherworld are intertwined and intuitively felt. The land, as elemental and as the sacred feminine, contains, supports, protects, provides for and teaches humanity.

Liminality

Brigit is generally referred to as a liminal goddess. She refuses to be defined and, as such, is a goddess for all and sundry. She was a mediator between the Fomorians and the Tuatha Dé Danann through her marriage to King Bres. She straddled two worlds as a mediator between pre-Christianity and Christianity. Saint Brigid embodied duality in her very conception – her father was a noble druid and her mother a bondmaid. She was born neither inside nor outside, neither at day nor at night, as told in the *Vita Prima* in chapter 6.3. Even in her sainthood, she was liminal between God and humanity. In her roles as a light-bringer and psychopomp, she serves as a mediator between life and death. She can enter the human world through birth and the Otherworld through death. She embodies both and, as such, dwells in the real and supernatural worlds.

According to folklore, fairies are believed to have the ability to cross the threshold between worlds. Tradition holds that at liminal times of the year, such as *Samhain* and *Bealtaine*, they move across the land, changing their location. Folk belief suggests fairies can move through the human world or watch from trees and rocks unseen. In these traditions, humans cannot enter the fairy realm at will, as they are rooted in the physical world. The contrast is clear: humans are portrayed as fixed beings, while the fairy folk, such as Brigit, are understood as liminal, which could be interpreted as evidence of her fairy essence.

Manifestation

The ability to manifest is the most remarkable ability that can be identified with Brigit as a lady of the Otherworld. Her ability to manifest in different times, spaces and locations is her supreme accomplishment. This ability sets her apart from all other gods and goddesses. As Brigantia, she manifested from the Celtic and classical worlds into the Irish Celtic world as Brigit. From Brigit, she manifested as Saint Brigid.

From Saint Brigid, she manifested into Maman Brigitte.

Within the Celtic goddess persona, one side of her presides over poetry. Ó hÓgáin considered poetry a verbal manifestation of mystical knowledge.[49]

Poets held high social prestige, considered experts almost equal to the druids. Many poets were said to receive their gifts of wisdom and fluency from otherworldly sources in adulthood. The goddess bestowed both material and mental well-being, while the fairies guarded secret lore.[50] Much of Irish poetic history features an inspiring otherworldly lady. This lady sometimes appears as a maiden to the poet while he composes or sleeps.[51] More often than not, Brigit is considered to manifest as the youthful maiden at *Imbolc* after her natural decay at *Samhain*.

Mantle

Brigid's green mantle is steeped in otherworldly magic. No story demonstrates this magic more than the tale of Brigid's cloak extending over the Curragh plains in County Kildare. When seeking land to build her convent, she asked a local chieftain for enough land. He agreed to give her as much land as her cloak would cover. At her will, the cloak extended and expanded over the plains until the chieftain begged her to stop. The story continues:

There was a king in the Curragh of Kildare long, long ago in the time of St Brigid. He had two horse ears, and he was so ashamed of them that he wore his hair very long to cover them. Anyone who cut the king's hair had to be put to death for fear the barber would reveal the secret. St Brigid shaved his hair and by a miracle when she had finished, the king put up his hand and found he had two ears like every other person. The king was so delighted that he said he would give Brigid anything she would ask. She said all she wanted was only as much land as her cloak would cover. She put the cloak on the ground and it spread and spread until a large part of the plain was covered. Here, she founded a church and a convent, and thousands came for alms, while those who were sick came to be cured.[52]

Milk

Milk and other dairy products are like gold dust to the fairies. Many stories exist in Irish folklore about fairies and milk. These stories range from fairies pushing young milkmaids after milking so that the milk pail will spill over. They are known to steal milk and butter from cows, particularly in May, the month of the fairies. They are known to bewitch cows, causing them to kick milk pails, produce no milk, or produce an abundance of milk. According to folklore, fairies wanted it for their supper.

Milk from cows was one of the earliest sacred foods throughout the world and an antidote to the poison of weapons. From the very outset, milk plays a significant role in Brigid's life. In the *Vita Prima*, Brigid was born as her mother crossed the threshold from outside to inside, carrying a pail of milk. Chapter six states that immediately the infant's body was washed with the warm milk she was carrying. As a child, Brigid was unable to stomach the food of the druid. In chapter eleven, Brigid is said to have vomited daily because of digesting the pagans' food. The druid declared, 'I am unclean, but this girl is filled with the holy spirit. She can't endure my food.' The druid chose a white cow and set it aside for the girl. A Christian woman milked the cow, and Brigid did not vomit it up, as her stomach had healed.

Miracles

Other miracles highlight Brigid's otherworldly abilities. In *The Life of Saint Brigid*, told by Cogitosus, upon receiving her veil, she knelt before an altar and touched the wooden base. At her touch, the wood flourished fresh and green. Another account tells how Brigid asked for help to reap the harvest. During their work, the heavens opened and it started pouring rain; yet, the workers, under her guidance, were kept dry as they continued to work. The same collection tells how she hung her wet clothes onto a sunbeam that shone through her window, as though it were a solid tree. In another story, she wrapped meat in her white cloak to bring to people experiencing poverty. Her cloak retained its white colour, without any stain. Cogitosus also tells how water from a river rose like a protective wall around thieves attempting to steal cattle. The cattle were able to escape, but not the thieves. Another tale recounts how a horse from a two-horse chariot breaks free while Brigid is in the chariot, praying in a meditative state. No harm comes to her as the hand of God takes the reins. Other stories tell of her miraculous abilities, including curing a man of his gluttony, dividing a steel chalice into three exactly equal parts by throwing it and replacing the vestments of the bishop after she had given them to the poor.

These miraculous stories, noted by Cogitosus, highlight Brigid's holiness and miraculous abilities. Impressive as they are, they are all told through the Christian lens. Christian virtues of generosity, charity, wisdom, humility and piety are to the fore in all stories about Brigid. Yet beneath the surface, a magician works wonders. At the surface level, her miracles stem from her faith and devotion to God. Below the surface, there is a strong current of mystery flowing to the Otherworld.

Night time

Nighttime is traditionally said to be when the fairy folk emerge. Those on the way home from fairs, pubs and visiting neighbours have often reported sighting the good people when everyone else was sleeping. Nighttime is not typically associated with Brigit; however, as a goddess, she was revered by the druids and poets. Druids and poets were often associated with magic and were believed to practice it, particularly at night. For the druids, night preceded day, and so night represents death and day represents life. Night and darkness were associated with the realm of the dead. The imagery of darkness in the lore of druid-poets, therefore, appears to have derived from this belief in inspiration from the Otherworld.[53]

Poetry

Irish folk legends tell of how poets and other individuals with magical powers received their skills as gifts from the fairies.[54] Brigit is the goddess of poetry, a most important art to the Celts. From early Irish glossaries, we read she, 'is then, the lady of poetry, the goddess that the poets used to worship, for very great and very noble was her care'.[55]

In Irish tradition, the poet was believed to possess mystical knowledge and his compositions were often regarded as possessing magical powers.[56] Dr Ó hÓgáin tells of a folk legend about a man with intellectual abilities who falls asleep by a mound. He dreams of a beautiful woman who comes to inspire him, even a book of wisdom, and when he awakens, he can compose verse without effort.[57]

Brigit, as a goddess, is often depicted with a fiery arrow of inspiration. Poetry, according to Ó hÓgáin, is like a maiden who appears to the poet as he composes; she is 'multiformed, multifaceted, multimagical, a noble well-clasped maiden'.[58] Poets were highly valued members of Irish Celtic society. The poet was originally a seer who expressed mystical insights in the form of rhetoric. The bard was considered a minor poet, whilst the *file* leaned more towards the meaning of seer.[59] It was assumed that the *file* possessed some of the capabilities of the druid, who ranked above even the king in societal terms. The bard and the *file* went to school to learn their craft, studying for up to twelve years. They had to master genealogies, antiquated traditions and the heroic tales, as well as develop their own magical skills. Training for poets was in oral form. Their master sang what had to be learned and the pupils in turn repeated it altogether. The pupils lay on their beds in a dark room, composing verses that their master later corrected. By lying in the dark, they are akin to the ancient druids, who sought wisdom from their ancestors in the darkness.[60] Poets played on the symbolism of darkness. Darkness cloaked their verse in mystery, enabling their reputation to thrive, as they possessed the magical ability to see what the vast majority of people could not.

The poet's most sacred, too, was his tongue. The tongue of the poets could divide poetry into *moladh agus aoir* (praise and satire). With his tongue, he could elevate a person's reputation with praise or destroy it with satire. He was handsomely paid for his praise by wealthy noblemen, yet also feared should he change his mind. The poet's most significant protection was his power of satire and the people's belief in it, as well as their fear of its consequences.[61] Those who were poets were considered to have mystical powers. They could rid themselves of rats, ghosts and cure illnesses with their verse.[62] They stood at a juncture between the physical and spiritual world. They were liminal. The ability of poets to use and understand language in such a way was seen as a gift from their goddess Brigit.

Brigit was and still is to this day a goddess of poetry. Brigit was the patroness of the poets and in her honour, the chief poet always carried a golden branch with tinkling bells, known as the *slat an draíochta* or rod of the druid.[63] Irish bards associated with the druids used a wand with gently twinkling bells. Druids made their wands of divination from the yew tree. They used their wands to control spirits, fairies, demons, elementals and ghosts.[64] Fairies are also associated with tinkling bells. Fairies are said to travel on white horses with manes braided and decorated with tinkling bells.

Entering the Otherworld before death required a passport. This was usually a silver branch of the sacred apple tree, given by the Celtic Fairy Queen to mortals willing to voyage to the Underworld in full human consciousness.

In addition to poetry, music played a vital role in

ancient Celtic life. Music is strongly associated with the Otherworld. Music, poetry and storytelling – the sacred trio of Irish Celtic life – were shared around the open hearth. This united communities and neighbours in their love for people and the arts, possibly also uniting the Otherworld and the human world. The atmosphere of a pub with an open fire during a music session or sing-along carries an otherworldly quality that seems to emanate from the performers. Ireland is an island of scholars, musicians, storytellers and poets. Perhaps Brigit, the *sídhe*, inspires and brings forth otherworldly artistic gifts.

Prophecy and Divination

The power of fire and the supernatural ability the smith was claimed to have had extended beyond the forge. A blacksmith was also supposed to be 'going with' the fairies. He was credited with an uncanny gift of prophecy and other extraordinary powers. His forge was located at a crossroads. He would often 'disappear' from his forge at specific periods. When he returned, he was able to tell his neighbours and clients about the secret happenings that had occurred to them or their families while he had been away. One story recounts how a blacksmith correctly prophesied that a man would get an inheritance from America, and for several others, the same blacksmith predicted calamities on certain days.[65]

Another story recounts how a man near a fort became lost and fell asleep within the fort. While he slept, it was said that he received the gift of prophecy from the fairies. He correctly prophesied that mass would cease to exist in his local parish and that he himself would die on a roadside on his way home.[66]

Brigit is the patroness goddess of seers, perceived as an expert in divination, prophecy, learning and poetry. The druids, of whom she was patroness, were well versed in the arts of seers and prophets. They could practice auguries, foretell the future and interpret nature. Ancient augury involved interpreting the flight patterns of birds. Birds embodied health, fertility and good fortune, which were all important to life sustenance.[67] Bird habits observed and interpreted included the croaking of ravens, the chirping of wrens and the flight of crows. Continental druids taught the doctrine of the transmigration of souls and practised divination of the future from auguries, especially from the raven.[68] The raven is and has been considered a magical, intelligent bird, associated with death and lost souls. To foretell the future, druids used astronomy and astrology. They searched for omens in human and animal sacrifices, which they conducted for divination.[69] The bull was commonly used as a means of divination, particularly its hide. The prophet wrapped himself in the hide of a newly slain bull and sat down by a waterfall or at the front of a precipice and meditated. Shortly after, the spirits would visit him and reveal to him what he wanted to know.

Druids interpreted dreams. Omen sticks called *coelbreni*, wands of trees such as hazel or yew, were cast upon the ground, and how they landed was interpreted. Druids also practised palm knowledge, which involved the druid chewing a specially prepared piece of meat and then entering a state of meditation, with his two palms placed against his cheeks.[70] Druidic sleep was another component of their magical abilities, which we now refer to as hypnosis.

Shapeshifting was a common feature of druidic magic, and it is said that druids could shapeshift themselves or others not only into alternative human states but also into animals.[71] What druids were capable of and what they worshipped in Brigit is an indication of the connection to magic and the supernatural.

Protectress

Folklore suggests that fairies are believed to protect the environment. They are said to protect the earth, the ecosystem and all its inhabitants. This nurturing aspect reportedly doesn't extend to humans. But Brigit is a protector of humans. Like the fairies, she protects the earth and animals, yet also humanity, particularly women, children and the marginalised.

Saint Brigid stood alongside people experiencing poverty and fought for the rights of women. Justice keepers were even called Brigit. Cogitosus recounts how a king had a rare and special fox that could perform tricks. The fox is accidentally killed by a man who presumed the fox to be wild. The man is sentenced to death by the king unless he can replace the dead fox with another of the same kind. It so happens that a wild fox comes to Brigid and shelters beneath her cloak. Brigid presents the fox to the king. The fox performs tricks equally as impressive as its predecessor. The king orders the release of the man and the fox runs back to the wild.

Protectress of women

In the *Life of Saint Brigid*, Cogitosus reports how a man gave a woman a silver brooch. Unbeknownst to her, he took it back and threw it in the ocean. He told her if she did not have the brooch, she would forever be his sex slave. The woman went to Brigid. A man approached the two women with a fish. When they cut open the fish, the brooch was inside, thus freeing the woman.

In another story, Cogitosus tells of Brigid helping a woman who had become pregnant through an illicit relationship. The woman, fearing shame and punishment, sought Brigid's help. Brigid blessed the woman and the pregnancy disappeared without childbirth or pain, saving the woman from social disgrace and possible death.

Rebirth

We are told that there is a close association between the concept of rebirth and that of the Otherworld.[72] Brigit the maiden returns to the world at *Imbolc* to begin her journey once more. Brigit is revered as the primary goddess of light and rebirth in Ireland and beyond.

Three

Triplism, as defined by Cunliffe, is an expression of extreme potency rather than any coming-together of three disparate elements.[73] This potency possibly explains all of Brigit's magical abilities and miraculous feats. She is a triple goddess, or one of the three Brigits. Brigid is surrounded by three animals, two oxen and a pig. There are three parts of the poet. From the heart of the poet flowed blood from the special vein, causing words to spring from the lungs, be retrieved in the head and be fashioned by the tongue as they entered the world.[74]

The poet, if justified in satire, could raise three blisters of shame on a person's face.[75] Pythagoras, the sixth-century philosopher, says it's a perfect number that is suggestive of the beginning, middle and end – a continuity. It could be linked to the tripartite division of early European society: farmers, warriors and clergy. As in the triple daughters and sons of the gods were for everyone. As the goddess of life, the number three suggests the shape of the pubic triangle, which is a symbol of reproduction. The original Trinity is the Triple Goddess. She was, she is, she will be.[76] Sculptures of deities with three heads, like the one found in Cavan, signify a heightened sense of sight, allowing them to look forward into the Otherworld and backwards into the human world.[77] Three in this context might also be indicative of Brigit's presence in three worlds: the pre-Christian world, the Christian world and the Otherworld of the fairies.

Water and Wells

For the Celts, water may have symbolised a connection to the underworld. Amongst other resorts, fairies were said to dwell beneath lakes.[78]

Water was always seen as a way of connecting to and communicating with the Otherworld.[79] The term 'well' also covers springs, deep areas in some rivers and streams and even standing water in hollowed-out rocks. Water in wells was observed to have originated from deep within the Earth. Wells, in particular, sprang up from the blood of a martyr or from the touch of a saint's or a fairy's staff.[80] Wells were also claimed to be linked to the Otherworld.[81] In Celtic times, springs and wells were often associated with divinities, particularly those related to healing cults.[82]

No goddess is as connected to healing as Brigit, especially in Ireland. Wells, in particular, are linked to Brigit. Stories told to us about Brigid's miraculous healing come from water or wells. In the *Vita prima*, Brigid transforms water from the well into beer and cures leprosy by sprinkling water. Her foster mother is healed when she drinks the beer changed by Brigid from water. Wells, like Brigit, are liminal. They link the upper and lower worlds. Common in traditional Irish storytelling is the *gruagach*, or wizard, who resides in a well. It was held that a deity was living on in the world of the dead underneath the well.[83]

'The burial mound like the well, and the sea, was regarded in Celtic belief as one of the entrances to the Otherworld'.[84] These goddesses associated with rivers and springs had special connections with cows.[85] A clear connection can be made between Brigit and the Otherworld. Sacred sites, such as the famous Brú na Boinne, were often located near water.

In Irish folklore, we read of the connections between fairies and wells:

> On a road called Cloone (na Cluain dara – oak trees in the vicinity) road joining two townlands there is a well called the 'Tocar'. On bright moonlight nights fairies were supposed in the long ago to be seen dancing around this well dressed as fairies were supposed to be dressed & drinking the water out of cups made out of dock leaves The water of this well is supposed to sparkle more brightly than the water of any well in the neighbourhood The cows grazing in the vicinity were supposed to thrive better when drinking water from this well. The people still use the water & seem to think there's a special virtue attached to the water. The water was supposed to cure stomach ills especially if taken fasting in the morning.[86]

Long before Christianity, Ireland's holy wells were revered as sacred springs and those that remain outside the Christian tradition today are known as fairy wells.[87]

In Ireland, it was believed that holy wells could be insulted by someone not treating them with due reverence, such as bathing animals in them, washing clothes, or urinating in them. The result, it was believed, would be that they would lose their curative powers and the damaging action would rebound on the inflictor.[88] Trees close to the wells were also considered off limits for any disrespectful behaviour. A story goes that beside three wells were three trees. A man wanted one of the trees. He asked the owner, but he refused to cut it down. He said he wouldn't do it, but if the man really wanted it, he could do it himself. At midnight, he returned with three men. Halfway through cutting it down, 'a light left the tree. A great noise was heard. They got terrified'.[89]

Another story in the National Folklore Collection recounts a stone covering a well in Cork, upon which Brigid herself was allegedly to have knelt and prayed. The well was never without water. The stone broke in half. Half of it remained above the well, the other half below. A protestant gentleman who was building a ditch put the stone into it. The next morning, he awoke to find it had vanished and was back in its original spot. And it has never been interfered with since.[90]

5

PLACES OF THE OTHERWORLD IN IRELAND ARE LINKED TO BRIGID

Ireland is home to many locations believed to possess strong spiritual energy and serve as portals to the Otherworld. Some of these sites are associated with Brigit, as they appear in both the myths of the goddess and the stories of Saint Brigid. The traditions describe landmarks where she manifested, performed miracles, or brought about abundance and growth. Folklore also speaks of wells dedicated to her that are said to offer access to the Otherworld. These places are among the key sacred locations in Ireland connected to Brigit.

Leinster

Leinster is the province most often associated with Brigit, both as a sovereign goddess and as a saint. It represents the union of her dual identities. In Kildare town, her pagan fire temple stands within the grounds of her church, a quiet reminder of Ireland's spiritual traditions before the coming of Christianity. It was in Kildare that Brigit founded

Ireland's first nunnery, which later became a double abbey for both monks and nuns.

Leinster was also a place of pilgrimage, where visitors came to seek Brigit's healing and wisdom. Historically, it was one of Ireland's five provinces, or *fifths*, extending from the River Liffey in Dublin. The province took its name from the *Laighean*, the dominant people of the region, whose ruling dynasty, the *Uí Dúnlainge*, was based on the plains of the River Liffey in County Kildare. The *Laighean* were believed to be of Celtic origin and were regarded as professional warriors, known variously as *Laigin*, *Gaileóin* or *Domnaind*.[1] Here in Leinster, they shared territory with the Fothairt. The Fothairt also held territory in modern Offaly near Croghan Hill.[2]

Hill of Allen

The midland region of Ireland, from Kildare west almost to the river Shannon, was anciently known as *Almhu* and at the eastern end of this was *Cnoc Almhain* or *Almu*. This hill rises to an impressive height of 206 metres above the Curragh plains, making it the highest point in county Kildare. The hill is situated in West Kildare beside the village of Allen. It is located at the easternmost point of the Bog of Allen, which gets its name from the hill. The top of the hill offers a remarkable view.

A small battlemented tower was erected there in

1859. In ancient times, the hill was a cultic site of the Leinstermen, dedicated to the god of light called by the Celtic name Vindos. The name of this deity developed into 'Fionn' in Irish, and he was reputed to have been a great seer and warrior. In the guise of Fionn Mac Cumhaill, he has become the most celebrated personage in all Irish lore. We are told that he had his residence on the hill and a small mound on the summit was still known until recently as his 'seat' (*Suí Finn*).[3]

According to legend, the base of the hill was used by Fionn Mac Cumhaill as a warrior training ground for his warriors.

No better place, then, for Brigit to appear to her Leinster men in *Cath Almaine* (Battle of Allen). The battle was a result of the High King demanding cattle tribute from the Leinstermen, but they refused. He called on the *Uí Néill*, the *Airghialla* and the *Connachta* tribes to invade the Laigín. On 11 December 722, on the hill of Allen, the hosts came together. 'Brighid showed herself over the hosts for the sake of the Laighin and Colm Cille showed himself over the hosts for the sake of the Uí Néill. Saint Brigid won the day'.[4]

The Curragh

To the south of the Hill of Allen lies the Curragh, known in medieval accounts as *Brigid's Pastures*.

Gerald of Wales described the plains as a place of remarkable abundance, writing that 'even though all the animals of the whole province have eaten the grass right down to the ground, when morning comes, they have just as much grass as ever'. This association with endless renewal reflects Brigit's enduring connection to fertility and sustenance. The vast green landscape, dotted with grazing sheep, continues to embody the sense of perpetual abundance attributed to her.

The Curragh also serves as the setting for the legend in which Saint Brigid is said to have miraculously acquired land for her monastery. Long regarded as sacred ground, it symbolises both spiritual and earthly vitality. The area is traditionally considered the heart of Leinster, where Brigit's pagan sanctuary is said to have evolved into her Christian church. Today, the Curragh remains a place of dualities: it sustains life through its rich pastures while also housing Ireland's Defence Forces and Training Centre. In this coexistence of fertility and warfare, life and death are held together beneath Brigit's symbolic green mantle.

Her wells

Wells were traditionally regarded as portals to the Otherworld. Ireland is said to have thousands of wells and according to Logan, fifteen of them are dedicated to Saint Brigid.[5]

Saint Brigid's Garden Well in Tully, Kildare, is a peaceful sanctuary dedicated to the saint. The gentle sound of flowing water fills the space, coming from an underground stream that passes beneath an arch carved with a Brigid's cross before reaching a modern bronze statue of Brigid. The stream flows through two stones known as St Brigid's Shoes before continuing onward. Beside the well stands a prayer tree where visitors tie *clooties*, small strips of cloth used in prayers for healing. Traditionally, the cloths were dipped into the well's waters and placed on the body before being tied to the tree. The garden's quiet atmosphere, surrounded by green fields, encourages reflection and devotion, echoing older traditions of pilgrimage.

Saint Brigid's Well at Kilcullenbridge offers a different setting. Smaller and located close to the main road, it is surrounded by a park decorated with fairy doors. The well appears to be less frequently visited and the site has a subdued, reflective quality compared to the Garden Well at Tully. Despite its modest appearance, it remains an integral part of the devotional landscape associated with Brigid in Kildare.

In contrast, Saint Brigid's Well at Liscannor, County Clare, has a powerful and more solemn atmosphere. It stands beside a graveyard said to contain the resting places of ancient kings and clan leaders. Visitors perform the traditional rounds before descending into the grotto, where the statue of Brigid is surrounded by offerings – photographs, candles and notes seeking her protection. The space carries a deep sense of reverence, symbolising both loss and renewal. Emerging from the grotto into the open air brings a renewed feeling of hope, reflecting Brigid's role as guardian of the living and the dead, and her enduring link to the Otherworld.

The well at Liscannor brings together Christian and pre-Christian traditions, representing a meeting point of earthly, spiritual and otherworldly realms. It stands as a potent example of Brigid's enduring presence in Ireland's sacred landscape.

Croghan Hill

The Fothairt, who shared territory with the Laigin in Kildare, also held territory in modern Offaly near Croghan Hill.[6]

Croghan Hill is the sacred inauguration hill of the Uí Failge sept of the *Laighean*. Like other elevated sites in Ireland, Croghan Hill is reminiscent of the assembly sites found throughout the country. Such elevated sites were most probably used for assemblies, fairs, markets and gatherings.[7]

Croghan Hill is situated to the east of Offaly and Kildare on territory known as the Bog of Allen. Croghan Hill is an isolated extinct volcano. 'The summit is topped by an earthen mound, seventy feet in diameter and about fifteen feet high.'[8] The hilltop cairn probably comes from the age of the passage-tomb builders of *Slieve na Cailligh* and the Boyne Valley.

Croghan was made famous by a discovery in 2003 by a machine driver who noticed a human body buried deep in the turf. These remains came to be known as Old Croghan man. It transpired that he had been tortured, cut in half and buried in the bog. Radiocarbon dating placed the time of death in the range of 362–175 BC. The wetlands had preserved and mummified the body. Archaeologists reported that such horrific executions were the fate for failed candidates for kingship in pre-Christian Ireland.

Legend has it that the sister of Queen Maeve, *Brí Éile*, is buried beneath the mound. She and her chariot are said to reside in the summit mound. An ancient poem called *Laoidh na Leacht* (Poem of the Monuments) describes the burial mound as the monument of Congal on the Hill of *Brí Éile*. The land below it was once known as *Móin Éile* (Bog of *Éile*), now anglicised into Bog of Allen. The mythical tale of 'The Boyhood Deeds of Fionn' refers to Croghan Hill as a 'fairy-mound' and recounts how the men of Ireland would travel to Croghan Hill at *Samhain* to woo a beautiful maiden whose palace was said to be beneath the hill. The hill was said to open at *Samhain*, the most opportune time of the year to access the Otherworld. The beautiful, otherworldly maiden associated with the hill is believed to have been *Brí Éile*.[9] However, Magan said that the old name for the hill was *Cruachán Brí Éile*. *Cruachán*, meaning a round-topped hill and *Brí*, possibly referring to Brigid.

It is attested chiefly that Saint Brigid was born at Faughart, Louth.[10] Others, such as Brian Wright and Noel Kissane, dispute Faughart as the Saint's birthplace, claiming that the widely held belief is due to the similarity between the name of the village and the name of the family to which she belonged, the Fothairt.

The Fothairt tribe had settled in places such as Offaly, Carlow, Wexford and Armagh. The specific branch of the Fothairt tribe to which Brigid was claimed was settled in the area of *Uí Fhailge*, Offaly, in the area east of Croghan Hill, Offaly, bordering County Kildare.[11]

Some claim that here on the bog of Derryarkin at the northern side of Croghan Hill, Saint Brigid came into the world, and not at Faughart, Louth. Regardless of being born here, it was on this hill that she also received her white veil from Bishop MacCaille.

Croghan Hill is said to embody Brigit's magical energy. At the place where she touched the altar, the wooden base is said to have taken root and continued to grow, flourishing ever since. The site later became renowned for its healing powers, believed to cure various afflictions and diseases. As Kenny notes, tales of Brigid's generosity, compassion and miraculous abilities spread throughout Ireland.[12] And it was from Croghan Hill, in County Offaly, where it all began.

The Bog of Allen, which lies at the base of Croghan Hill, was called the 'Notorious Red Bog of Ely' by surveyor and cartographer Sir William Petty in 1657.[13]

Croghan Hill has long been associated with Brigid and the Otherworld. The hill's atmosphere, particularly on mist-filled mornings, lends itself to a sense of mystery and sacred presence. The path to the summit is steep but short, and along the way lies a small, distinctive graveyard. The irregular shapes and placements of the headstones, enclosed by stone walls and overlooking the surrounding boglands, give the site a uniquely mystical quality.

Near the summit stands a carved stone bearing an image of Brigid and the inscription, 'Brigid removed McCaille's veil and wrote her own narrative of hope'. This inscription evokes Brigid's independence and her blending of Christian and pre-Christian traditions, symbolising the union of earthly and otherworldly realms. The view from the hilltop opens across the surrounding countryside, a landscape long believed to hold traces of her presence and power.

Newgrange

Among Ireland's otherworldly landscapes, *Brú na Bóinne* and Rathcroghan stand out as primary centres of myth and spiritual significance. Although no clear link exists between Brigit and Rathcroghan, a strong connection binds her to Newgrange. The passage grave at Newgrange was regarded as a place of continued life, where fire – and possibly Brigit, in her role as psychopomp – guided the spirits of the dead into the Otherworld. Like other passage graves, Newgrange served as a resting place for the dead and for ancestors, yet it held particular importance as the burial site of the kings of the Tuatha Dé Danann.[14] In mythology, one of these kings was the Dagda, Brigit's father and ruler of the *sídhe*.

Brigit's association with Newgrange also extends through her mother, Boann, whose presence endures in the landscape as the River Boyne. *Brú na Bóinne* refers to the more expansive passage-tomb complex encompassing Newgrange, Dowth and Knowth. Situated north of the Boyne, the name translates as 'womb of Boann' or 'womb of the White Cow'. Boann and Brigit are often viewed as overlapping figures and in some traditions, they are described as mother and daughter.

Constructed over 5,000 years ago, Newgrange is associated with the Dagda and the goddess Boann, as well as the Morrígan, who is also identified in certain traditions as Brigit's mother. The mound, approximately 100 metres in diameter and 15 metres high, contains a long passage leading to a cruciform chamber with three recesses, each holding a granite basin thought to have contained cremated remains of chieftains. Above the entrance lies a 'roof box' through which the rising sun at the winter solstice illuminates the inner passage and chamber. This solar alignment symbolised renewal and the transference of life, as the nurturing sun carried the spirits of the dead into the Otherworld, ensuring continued prosperity for the living.

The Dagda, his son Oenghus and Brigit each bear solar attributes. When the Celts arrived in Ireland in the final centuries BCE, they adopted Newgrange as the dwelling of their great father deity, the sun-like Dagda.[15] According to Ó hÓgáin, the Celts regarded Newgrange as a fairy palace, the home of the supreme fairy king – the Dagda himself.[16]

In the *Metrical Dindshenchas*, Newgrange is described as a fairy mound built by the 'harsh Dagda'. In the *Gabáil int Síde* (The Taking of the *Síde*), the Dagda is named as the owner of Newgrange, while in *Tochmarc Étaíne* (The Wooing of Étaín), it is Elcmar, husband of Boann, who is said to reside there. Regardless of ownership, it was Oenghus, the pre-Celtic god of the sun and son of the Dagda and Boann, who ultimately claimed Newgrange for himself by outwitting his father.

Oenghus represents renewal and the return of life after the stillness of winter. His birth, said to have occurred when time stood still, mirrors Brigit's own associations with rebirth and seasonal transition. Although rarely linked in Irish folklore, both figures share the Dagda as their father and embody themes of light, life and regeneration.

Visitors to Newgrange cannot fail to be struck by the uniqueness of the site. The great mound, overlooking the Boyne Valley, exudes a strong yet tranquil energy. Inside, the corbelled roof remains perfectly intact since its construction around 3200 BC. The most remarkable feature is the roof box above the entrance, designed to channel the light of the rising sun along the passage and into the inner chamber at sunrise on the winter solstice. During tours, this alignment is recreated artificially, offering a glimpse of the extraordinary spectacle that occurs naturally once a year, illuminating the chamber in golden light.

The *Cailleach*

The *Cailleach* and Brigit are often regarded as two opposing aspects of the same spirit. They share several characteristics that reflect the cyclical balance between life and death, winter and spring. A reference to the *Cailleach* appears in Leinster, where she is known as *Cailleach Laigen*. In Kildare, she is associated with an inauguration site called the 'Chair of Kildare'. It was said that she possessed the power to heal sick cattle and to restore butter that had been stolen.[17]

If the *Cailleach* and Brigit are regarded as two aspects of the same spirit, many sites across Ireland are associated with the *Cailleach*. These include her cairn on Slieve Gullion in Armagh, the Hag's Head on the Cliffs of Moher in Clare, the Hag's Chair at Loughcrew in Meath, the Hag's Face at Coulagh Bay in West Cork and her dwelling off Dursey Island, formerly known as *Oileáin Baoí*.

The locations associated with the *Cailleach* remain integral to Ireland's mythological landscape, reflecting the enduring link between the two figures.

6

CONNECTING WITH BRIGIT AS LADY OF THE IRISH OTHERWORLD

Brigit, as a fairy woman, doesn't generally appear in many conversations, yet it's a side of her that has always been present in Irish tradition.

Irish folklore speaks of an Otherworld – a realm that runs in parallel to our own natural world. Within traditional belief systems, this concept is fathomable and even logical. Many reasons have been proposed to support the possibility of such a realm, rather than dismiss its existence. Interest in the spirit world and in the fairy realm has existed in Irish culture for as long as can be remembered. Stories of encounters with beings that were, however, unwelcome have been documented throughout history. These accounts demonstrate how supernatural beings were believed to move freely in the world, often unnoticed by humans, until they chose to reveal themselves.

For the most part, beings from the Otherworld were not thought to come knocking for attention. They didn't really like humans and, as such, didn't wish to interact with them. At times, though, the bold ones would push the boat out, appearing to those who not only believed but were also sensitive to energy changes, glimpses out of the corner of the eye, or a high-pitched voice speaking in tongues.

The National Folklore Collection contains many examples of how people endeavoured to show respect for fear of the fairy folk. Fairies were said to take children from the cradle if anyone had interfered with their raths or homes. However, not all of them were considered entirely bad. They were called 'the good people', 'good neighbours' and 'good folk' for a reason. Believed to have the power to do both good and bad, the people of yesteryear tried to maintain good terms with them.[1]

In Irish tradition, the natural world is not merely landscape but a living threshold where the human and the Otherworld meet. Healing, restoration and communion with the divine take place within this realm of streams, stones and sacred groves. It is here that the veil thins and where beings of the *sídhe* are believed to move unseen through wind, water and root.

Hermits and seers once sought such places for solitude and inspiration, living at the margins of society much like the fairies themselves. Removed from the noise of daily life, they listened to the voice of the land – a voice that carried wisdom, warning and renewal. In these wild sanctuaries, the boundaries between human spirit and Otherworld consciousness dissolved, allowing for an authentic connection to the source to be restored.

Traditional belief holds that nature spirits dwelling in trees, wells, mountains and rivers can teach patience, resilience and respect for the cycles of life. Their lessons remind humanity to take only what is needed and to honour the sanctity of every living thing.

Perhaps if the land were treated with greater care – if sacred places were respected rather than exploited, and if nature were once again regarded as sentient – the fairies of the Otherworld might draw closer to human awareness. The vitality of the earth and the presence of the divine have always been entwined, and through the fairies, this connection is remembered.

Brigit, as *Bean Feasa* (wise woman), *Bean Ghlúine* (midwife) and *Bean Chaointe* (keener), embodies the healer, manifester and mourner. Through these forms, she guides transformation, renewal and communion between the worlds.

Those who feel called to connect with Brigit as Fairy Queen and Lady of the Otherworld often include healers, herbalists, artists, poets, death doulas, and all who move between spiritual and material realities. Such individuals may seek her guidance in moments of change – birth, death, creation or release – when boundaries between the visible and invisible grow thin.

Connection with Brigit in her fairy aspect begins with reverence. A respectful and intentional relationship can be cultivated through daily acknowledgement – a whispered prayer, an offering, or mindful awareness of her presence in the natural world. Her aspect as Fairy Woman invites communication with the spirits of land, water and air, those who share the earth yet belong to the unseen realms.

Spaces dedicated to her may incorporate the colours green, red and white, which symbolise the Otherworld, alongside natural elements such as crystals, herbs and stones. An invocation may begin:

Queen of the Fae,
Queen of the Sídhe,
Bride – Brighde,
I call to thee.

Through ritual, intention and word, devotion to Brigit becomes a bridge to the Otherworld. Whether within the home or outdoors, honouring her acknowledges the life that animates both seen and unseen realms. Traditional offerings of milk, honey, or butter left at wells, gardens, or sacred trees express gratitude and strengthen this bond.

Sacred places – from local holy wells to ancient sites such as Glastonbury Tor and Tintagel – are often imbued with her energy. At such thresholds, the veil between worlds is said to be thinnest, allowing her presence as Fairy Queen and keeper of otherworldly fire to be most keenly felt.

Imbolc marks Brigit's most powerful threshold moment, when she is said to return from the Otherworld bringing renewal to land and life. Accompanied by her white, red-eared cow – an otherworldly creature – she blesses growth and rebirth. At this time, ancient customs of honouring both Brigit and the *sí* (fairy folk) merge, reaffirming the bond between humanity, nature and the unseen world.

When milking a cow, the first drops were traditionally poured onto the ground, or a cross was traced on the animal's side with a thumb dipped in the foam of fresh milk.[2] Not everyone today keeps cattle or works the land, yet the sentiment behind these customs can still be honoured in modern ways. A quiet blessing may be offered when opening milk, cream, or any other dairy liquid – a small act of gratitude that preserves the spirit of the tradition.

At *Samhain*, potatoes on the first night of November were set aside on a saucer for the fairies.[3] On Halloween night, the fairies were believed to be on the move. To keep relations sweet, the table was often left set all night with plenty of food, or people would go for a mug of tea and a slice of bread by the fire.[4]

Practices in Irish homes included hanging a horseshoe above the door for good luck. Women were known to place a thong in a baby's cradle to prevent the fairies from taking the child.[5]

The *Creideamh sí*, or fairy faith, concerned itself with what was important: food and children, providing bread and butter on the table, the secrets of nature and herbs to promote health and well-being, and good law to foster a stable society.[6] Maintaining good relations with the Tuatha Dé Danann was crucial to ensure the fertility of the land, its people and their livestock. These ancestral values still hold meaning today, reminding humanity that nourishment, shelter and love are sacred necessities. The faith once placed in the Tuatha Dé Danann for these blessings continues through customs honouring Brigit, Lady of the Irish Otherworld.

Elements of *creideamh sí* appear in *Imbolc* traditions dedicated to her. This festival celebrates abundance and the returning light after winter. Holy wells and sacred sites connected to Brigit are visited – offerings are made and prayers are spoken for renewal and blessing. Indoors, spaces are cleansed in preparation for her arrival – fires are kindled or candles lit to invite her warmth. In older times, new straw bedding was laid for animals and meals were prepared for hungry spirits or travellers – symbolising generosity between worlds. Typical foods included oat bread, potatoes, cally, or boxty, with regional variations across Ireland.

To invoke Brigit's healing power, a *Brat Bhríde* – a piece of cloth – was left outside overnight for her to bless as she passed. In Cork, a linen cloth was laid on a hedge overnight, awaiting her touch or blessing as she journeyed westward. Such beliefs elevate her to the realm of fairy goddesses, like Áine, a fairy goddess said to return on the eve of the summer solstice to celebrate her own rites.[7]

A *Brídeog* doll, crafted from straw, twigs, or cloth, is part of an ancient custom still practised in some parts of Ireland. Traditionally, children made a *Brídeog* for St Brigid's Day, creating the doll as a physical representation of Brigid.

At *Samhain*, though not traditionally her festival, Brigit's lamenting aspect as *Bean Chaointe* may be honoured. The season invites remembrance. Through the act of the *keen*, her presence gives voice to what is sacred – allowing pain and memory to be expressed and released, offering renewal at this threshold between worlds.

Conclusion

Brigit's role as Lady of the Irish Otherworld reflects her deep connection to the supernatural and fairy realms of Ireland. Across the landscape, countless beings of the *sídhe* are said to dwell in rivers, wells, trees, bogs, mountains, and beneath ancient mounds that hide their radiant palaces. These entities vary in form and temperament, often known only within local traditions.

Among them, two figures may be witnessed with Brigit: the *Leannán Sí* and the *Bean Sí*. Lady Wilde described the *Leannán Sí* as the inspirer of poets and musicians, mirroring Brigit's role as patroness of poetry and creative vision. The *Bean Sí*, whose keening announces death and transition, echoes Brigit's ancient aspect as *Bean Chaointe*, the first and archetypal keener of Ireland. Brigit is also linked with healing fairies and the *Bean Feasa*, wise women of leechcraft and spiritual guidance who once served their communities in times of illness and uncertainty.

In Celtic tradition, the smith held sacred status, embodying transformation through fire and darkness. Brigit's identity as a divine smith reinforces her association with the creative and regenerative powers of the Otherworld.

Though known for her light, dawn and the returning warmth of *Imbolc*, Brigit also holds dominion over darkness, death and rebirth. Her dual nature mirrors that of the *Cailleach*, the Crone of winter and decay, suggesting that both may be opposing faces of one being. Brigit's lament was said to be the first keen in Ireland, a cry that signified both loss and renewal. As a psychopomp, she guided souls into the Otherworld and presided over fire, tombs and thresholds – the sacred spaces of release and transformation.

Death was understood as the natural passage into the Otherworld, and Brigit's enduring presence embodies this eternal cycle. Her many forms – goddess, saint, *Maman Brigitte*, *Brigantia* – reveal a spirit capable of endless transformation while remaining constant in essence.

Brigit shares traits with Irish fairy queens such as Áine, Aoibheall and Clíodhna, all of whom are associated with sunlight, prophecy and the triadic pattern of power. Yet unlike these queens, who often retreated into subterranean realms, Brigit rose into sainthood within Christian Ireland. Though her associations with death, war and prophecy were softened, they remained at the heart of her character.

Her genealogy further anchors her within the Otherworld. Her father, the Dagda, king of the *sídhe*, ruled fertility and abundance. Her brother, Finnbhearra, was the fairy king of Connacht. Through her mother, she may be connected to Boann or the Morrígan, both linked to the sacred white cow with red ears – a recurring emblem of the Otherworld in Brigit's lore.

Animals appear throughout her stories: cows, dogs, sheep, horses, boars, wolves, foxes, ducks and bees. Her ability to communicate with and calm these creatures reflects a profound harmony between the human and nonhuman worlds, a trait shared by other fairy queens.

The colours red, white and green – long associated with Brigit and the fairies – express her enduring connection to the Otherworld. Tales of Saint Brigid often mention the white cow with red ears, a sign of those who cross between mortal and immortal realms.

Brigit's miracles – acts of healing, prophecy and manifestation – reveal powers that transcend the boundaries of nature. Her gift of *imbas*, or divine inspiration, aligns her closely with the *Leannán Sí* and other muses of the Otherworld who inspire poets, seers and visionaries.

Sacred sites dedicated to Brigit across Ireland are often regarded as portals to the unseen. Wells consecrated to her, whether in her guise as goddess or saint, continue to draw pilgrims seeking healing, blessing and communion with the departed. These wells, gateways to the Otherworld, affirm her enduring role as mediator between the living and the divine.

Brigit's spirit is one of perpetual transformation. Originating as an elemental presence of the land, she evolved into a mother goddess and later a saint, reflecting the spiritual growth of those who honoured her. Her fluidity reveals how sacred archetypes adapt to human consciousness while remaining timeless in essence.

The *sídhe* once held a central place in Irish belief, but as religion and culture changed, their veneration faded. Restoring Brigit's otherworldly origins restores balance between the seen and the unseen, reminding the modern world of the value of ancestral wisdom.

Each of Brigit's forms expresses a facet of her vast nature. As Fairy Woman, she calls to those who move between worlds – healers, midwives, poets, shamans, death doulas and all who sense the unseen. Even for those rooted in the physical world, she remains a guide toward renewal, creativity and reverence for all life.

Brigit transcends categorisation. Her essence unites the goddess, the saint, the elemental and the fairy queen. Through her fluidity, she embodies evolution, compassion and harmony among all beings – qualities that humanity needs now more than ever. As Lady of the Irish Otherworld, she endures as a muse, healer and guardian of the threshold, an eternal light that bridges worlds

Endnotes

Introduction

1. Farrelly, J., *Farrelly's Field Guide to Irish Faerie Folk* (O'Brien Press, 2024).
2. MacKillop, J., *Dictionary of Celtic Mythology* (Oxford University Press, 2006).
3. Houlihan, M., *Irish Fairies, A short History of the Sidhe* (Independently published, 2022).
4. O'Brien, L., *Fairy Faith in Ireland* (Eel and Otter Press, 2021).
5. Magan, M., *Listen to the land speak: A journey into the wisdom of what lies beneath us* (Gill, 2022).
6. Wentz, W.E., *The Fairy-faith in Celtic countries* (Oxford University Press, 1966).
7. https://www.duchas.ie, CBÉS 1119, p. 141.
8. https://www.duchas.ie, CBÉS 0250, p. 309.
9. Apffel-Marglin, F., *Subversive spiritualities: How rituals enact the world* (Oxford University Press, 2011).
10. Ó hÓgáin, D., *The sacred isle: belief and religion in pre-Christian Ireland* (Boydell Press 1999).
11. *Ibid.*
12. *Ibid.*
13. Condit, T., and Cooney, G., 'Heritage Guide No. 8: Newgrange, Co. Meath: Neolithic Religion and the Midwinter Sunrise', *Archaeology Ireland* (Wordwell Ltd., 1999).
14. Harbison, P., *Pre-Christian Ireland: From the First Settlers to the Early Celts* (Thames and Hudson, 1988).
15. Condit and Cooney, *Heritage Guide No. 8*.
16. Mackillop, J., *A dictionary of Celtic mythology* (Oxford University Press, 2006).
17. Houlihan, *Irish Fairies*.
18. Ó hÓgáin, *The sacred isle*.
19. *Ibid.*
20. Wentz, *The Fairy-faith in Celtic countries*.
21. MacKillop, *Dictionary of Celtic Mythology*.
22. Wentz, *The Fairy-faith in Celtic countries*.
23. *Ibid.*

24. Wilde, L., *Ancient Legends of Ireland* (Hobby Horse, 1887).
25. Lenihan, E., *Meeting the Other Crowd* (Gill Books, 2003).
26. Houlihan, *Irish Fairies*.
27. Ó hÓgáin, *The sacred isle*.
28. *Ibid*.

The *Sí* and Brigit

1. Ó hÓgáin, D., *Myth, Legend, & romance: an encyclopaedia of the Irish folk tradition* (Collins Press, 1990).
2. https://www.duchas.ie, CBÉS 0789, p. 123.
3. Heaney, M., *Over Nine Waves: A Book of Irish Legends: The Reign of Bres* (Faber & Faber, 1994).
4. Kelly, E.P., *Brigid: Pagan Goddess and Christian Saint* (https://www.academia.edu/Documents/in/Irish_Goddess_Brigid, *Irish Lives Remembered*, 53, Summer 2021).
5. MacCulloch, J.A., *Religion of the ancient Celts* (Routledge, 2014).
6. *Ibid*.
7. *Ibid*.
8. Ó Duinn, S., *Where three streams meet: Celtic Spirituality*. (Columba Press, 2000).
9. MacCulloch, *Religion of the ancient Celts*.
10. Ó Duinn, *Where three streams meet*.
11. Ó hÓgáin, *Myth, Legend, & romance*.
12. MacCulloch, *Religion of the ancient Celts*.
13. Wentz, *The Fairy-faith in Celtic countries*.
14. *Ibid*.
15. Ó hÓgáin, D., *The Lore of Ireland* (Collins Press, Cork, 2006).
16. Wentz, *The Fairy-faith in Celtic countries*.
17. O'Brien, *Fairy Faith in Ireland*.
18. Wentz, *The Fairy-faith in Celtic countries*.
19. MacCulloch, *Religion of the ancient Celts*.
20. Ó Duinn, *Where three streams meet*.
21. *Ibid*.
22. MacKillop, *A dictionary of Celtic mythology*.
23. O'Brien, *Fairy Faith in Ireland*.
24. Daimler, M., *Pagan Portals – Fairy Queens: Meeting the Queens of the Otherworld* (John Hunt Publishing, 2019).
25. Ó hÓgáin, *Myth, Legend, & romance*.

26. Gregory, L., *Gods and Fighting Men: The Story of the Tuatha De Danaan and of the Fianna of Ireland*, arranged and put into English (BoD–Books on Demand, 2024).
27. MacCulloch, *Religion of the ancient Celts*.
28. Gregory, *Gods and Fighting Men*.
29. Dinneen, P.S., *An Irish-English Dictionary: Being a Thesaurus of Words, Phrases and Idioms of the Modern Irish Language, with Explanations in English*. (For the Irish texts society by MH Gill & son, Limited, 1904).
30. MacKillop, *A dictionary of Celtic mythology*.
31. Daimler, M., *Pagan Portals – Fairy Queens: Meeting The Queens of the Otherworld* (John Hunt Publishing, 2019).
32. Daimler, M., *Pagan Portals –Aos Sidhe: Meeting the Irish Fair Folk* (John Hunt Publishing, 2022).
33. Ó Duinn, *Where three streams meet*.
34. Daimler, *Pagan Portals – Fairy Queens*.
35. MacCulloch, *Religion of the ancient Celts*.
36. Ó hÓgáin, *The Lore of Ireland*.
37. Ó hÓgáin, *The sacred isle*.
38. Ó hÓgáin, *The Lore of Ireland*.
39. Sjoestedt, M.L., *Celtic Gods and Heroes*. (Courier Corporation, 2000).
40. Carmody, I.. *The Dagda and the Mór Rígain in Cath Maige Tuired from Harp, Club and Cauldron*. Retrieved from https://www.academia.edu/42767242/
41. Ross, A., *Everyday life of the pagan Celts* (Batsford, 1970).
42. Vučković, A., *Dagda, Potbellied Chief Deity of the Celtic Pantheon*, 2019. Retrieved from https://www.ancient-origins.net/myths-legends/dagda-0012548.
43. Ó Duinn, *Where three streams meet*.
44. Fraser, J., *The first battle of Moytura* (Royal Irish Academy, 1916).
45. *Metrical Dindsenchas*, vol. 3, poem 3, *Boand*, CELT (Corpus of Electronic Texts, a project .of University College Cork).
46. Daimler, M., *Pagan Portals – The Dagda*.
47. Carmody, *The Dagda and the Mór Rígain*.
48. Kelly, F., *A guide to early Irish law* (Dublin Institute for Advanced Studies, 1988).
49. Wentz, *The Fairy-faith in Celtic countries*.
50. Ó hÓgáin, *The Lore of Ireland*.

51. Anonymous. *Cath Maige Tuired: The Second Battle of Mag Tuired.* Translated by Elizabeth A. Gray. CELT: The Corpus of Electronic Texts at University College Cork, T300010. https://celt.ucc.ie/published/T300010/index.html.
52. Croker, T.C., *Fairy legends and traditions of the south of Ireland* (William Tegg, 1862).
53. *Ibid.*
54. Ó Duinn, *Where three streams meet.*
55. Ó hÓgáin, *The sacred isle.*
56. *Ibid.*
57. MacCulloch, *Religion of the ancient Celts.*

The Otherworld of Ireland
1. Wentz, *The Fairy-faith in Celtic countries.*
2. Magan, M., *Listen to the land speak: A journey into the wisdom of what lies beneath us* (Gill, 2022).
3. Daimler, M., *Pagan Portals – Aos Sidhe.*
4. *Ibid.*
5. van Hamel, A.G. ed., *Immrama* (Vol. 10), (Dublin Institute for Advanced Studies, 1941).
6. Mac Cana, P., *Celtic Mythology.* Hamlyn, UK, 1970).
7. *Ibid.*
8. Wentz, *The Fairy-faith in Celtic countries.*
9. MacKillop, *A dictionary of Celtic mythology.*
10. Ross, *Everyday life of the pagan Celts.*
11. *Ibid.*
12. Ó hÓgáin, *The sacred isle.*
13. Mac Cana, *Celtic Mythology.*
14. Green, M.J., *Celtic Myths* (University of Texas Press, 1993).
15. Gimbutas, M., *The Living Goddesses* (University of California Press, 2001).
16. Harbison, P., 1988. *Pre-Christian Ireland: From the First settlers to the Early Celts.* (Thames and Hudson, 1988).
17. Green, *Celtic Myths.*

Death, The Otherworld and Brigit
1. Gimbutas, *The Living Goddesses.*
2. Green, *Celtic Myths.*
3. Croker, *Fairy legends and traditions.*

4. *Ibid.*
5. Kelly, 'Brigid: Pagan Goddess and Christian Saint'.
6. Hutton, R., *Queens of the wild: pagan goddesses in Christian Europe: an investigation* (Yale University Press, 2022).
7. Murphy, G., 1952. *The lament of the old woman of Beare.* Proceedings of the Royal Irish Academy. Section C: Archaelogy, Celtic Studies, History, Linguistics, Literature, 1952).
8. Ó hÓgáin, D., *Myth, legend, & romance: an encyclopædia of the Irish folk tradition* (Ryan, 1990).
9. Murphy, 'The lament of the old woman of Beare'.
10. Stokes (2001), (2008) *On the Life of Saint Brigid*, CELT Text T201010, p. 65 (Corpus of Electronic Texts, a project of University College Cork).
11. Ó hÓgáin *Myth, legend, & romance.*
12. The earliest literary mention appears in the twelfth-century satire 'Vision of Mac Conglinne', where she is called 'White Nun of Beare' (Caillech Bérre bán); hhttps://celt.ucc.ie/published/T308002.html
13. Ó hÓgáin, *Myth, legend, & romance.*
14. Hutton, *Queens of the wild: pagan goddesses.*
15. McIntyre, M., 2013 *The Cailleach Bheara*. Retrieved from: http://www.academia.edu/6088609/The_Cailleach_Bheara_A_Study_Of_Scottish_Highland_Folklore_in_Literature_and_Film
16. Hutton, *Queens of the wild: pagan goddesses.*
17. Ó hÓgáin, *Myth, legend, & romance.*
18. Murphy, 'The lament of the old woman of Beare'.
19. *Ibid.*
20. Ó Crualaoich, G., *The Book of the Cailleach* (Cork University Press, 2006).
21. Eleanor Hull, 'Legends and Traditions of the Cailleach Bheara or Old Woman (Hag) of Beare', *Folklore* 38, no. 3 (1927): 225–254 Taylor & Francis OnlineAcademia.edu; This is the seminal academic article on the subject. Hull specifically notes that the blessed veil worn by the Cailleach is 'a Christian appropriation of her hood, for, as in many other cases, the pagan goddess reappears in later days as a Christian nun.
22. MacKenzie, D.A., *Wonder Tales from Scottish Myth &*

Legend (Blackie and son, Limited, 1917).
23. *Ibid.*
24. Stokes (2004), (2010), *The Second Battle of Moytura*, CELT Text T300011, p. 95–97 (Corpus of Electronic Texts, a project of University College Cork).
25. Bourke, A., 1988. *Working and Weeping: Women's Oral Poetry in Irish and Scottish Gaelic* (UCD, School of Social Justice, Women's Studies, 1988).
26. MacKillop, *A dictionary of Celtic mythology*.
27. Kelly, E.P., *Brigid: Pagan Goddess and Christian Saint; Irish Lives Remembered*, 53 (Summer 2021), p. 7 (Digital magazine, produced by Irish Family History Centre (via publisher Eneclann).
28. Kelly, E.P., *Brigid: goddess, druidess and saint* (The History Press. 2011).
29. Stokes (2004), (2010), CELT Text T300011, p. 97 (Corpus of Electronic Texts, a project of University College Cork)
30. *Ibid.*, p. 95
31. Green, *Celtic Myths*.
32. Ballard, L.M., *The good people: New fairylore essays* (University Press of Kentucky, 1991).
33. https://www.duchas.ie (CBÉS 0963 033; https://www.duchas.ie/en/cbes/5044784/5037758/5081789?HighlightText=a+small+wee+woman+all+in+white&Route=stories&SearchLanguage=ga
34. https://www.duchas.ie CBES 0721, p. 199
35. https://www.duchas.ie CBÉS 0794, p. 99
36. https://www.duchas.ie CBÉS, 0682, p.133
37. Lysaght, *The Banshee*.
38. Briggs, K.M., *The fairies in tradition and literature*. (Psychology Press, 2002).
39. MacKillop, *A dictionary of Celtic mythology*.
40. Lysaght, *The Banshee*.
41. *Ibid.*
42. *Ibid.*
43. Kelly, Brigid: *Pagan Goddess and Christian Saint*.
44. MacKillop, *A dictionary of Celtic mythology*.
45. Weber, C., *Brigid: History, Mystery, and Magick of the Celtic Goddess* (Weiser Books, 2015).
46. *Annals of Tigernach*, s.a. 596 (Stokes, RC 17, p. 174);

https://celt.ucc.ie/published/T100002A.html; Whitley Stokes (ed. & trans.), 'The Annals of Tigernach', *Revue Celtique* 17 (1896), p. 174 (year 596).
47. Connolly, S., *Vita Prima Sanctae Brigitae.*
48. Stoker, W., *The Battle of Allen* (translation). *Revue Celtique* 24, 1903).

Brigit's Otherworldly Abilities
1. Hutton, *Queens of the wild: pagan goddesses.*
2. Cogitosus, *Life of St Brigit.*
3. Connolly, S., *Vita Prima Sanctae Brigitae.*
4. *Bethu Brigte*, author unknown. Retrieved from https://celt.ucc.ie/published/T201002.)
5. Cogitosus, *Life of St Brigit.*
6. Cusack, C., *Brigit: Goddess, Saint, 'Holy Woman', and Bone of Contention* (Sydney Studies in Religion, 2007).
7. Kissane, N., *Saint Brigid of Kildare: life, legend and cult.* Open Air, 2017).
8. Cogitosus, *Life of St Brigit.*
9. *Ibid.*
10. Ó hÓgáin, *Myth, legend, & romance.*
11. MacKillop, *A dictionary of Celtic mythology.*
12. Wright, B., *Brigid: goddess, druidess and saint* (The History Press, 2011).
13. Houlihan, *Irish Fairies.*
14. Wright, *Brigid: goddess, druidess and saint*
15. Lysaght, *The Banshee:*
16. MacKillop, *A dictionary of Celtic mythology.*
17. Ó hÓgáin, *Myth, legend, & rom.ance.*
18. Kissane, *Saint Brigid of Kildare.*
19. Condren, M., T*he Serpent and the Goddess: Women, Religion, and Power in Celtic Ireland (Harper and Row,* 1987)
20. Kelly, E. P., *The Enchanted Cow in Irish Tradition.* Irish Lives Remembered, 48, 2020), p. 11 ((Digital magazine, produced by Irish Family History Centre via publisher Eneclann).
21. *Betha Bhrighde* (*Book of Lismore* recension), quoted and translated by Proinsias Mac Cana, *Celtic Mythology* (1970), as the female is an emissary from the Otherworld.
22. Kelly, *The Enchanted Cow*

23. *Ibid.*
24. Ó hÓgáin, *The sacred isle.*
25. Wright, *Brigid: goddess, druidess and saint*
26. Ó hÓgáin, *The sacred isle.*
27. *Ibid.*
28. *Ibid.*
29. Green, *Celtic Myths.*
30. Ó hÓgáin, *Myth, legend, & romance.*
31. Kissane, *Saint Brigid of Kildare.*
32. Cambrensis, G. *Expugnatio Hibernica: Conquest of Ireland* (A. B. Scott & F. X. Martin, Eds; Vol. 3). Royal Irish Academy. http://www.jstor, 1978).
33. https://www.joeheaney.org/en/prayer-for-raking-the-fire/
34. MacKillop, *A dictionary of Celtic mythology.*
35. Danaher, K., *In Ireland Long Ago* (Mercier Press, 1964).
36. https://www.duchas.ie, CBÉS 0364, p. 122
37. https://www.duchas.ie, CBÉS 0263, p. 150
38. Ellis, P.B., *The Druids.* Eerdman's Publishing Company, 1994).
39. MacCulloch, *Religion of the ancient Celts.*
40. Pliny, G.S., (Pliny The Elder) *Natural History* (Penguin Classics, Reprint 1991).
41. https://www.duchas.ie, dúchas.ie, CBÉS 0239, p. 332
42. https://www.duchas.ie,, CBÉS 0883, p. 114
43. Ó hÓgáin, *Myth, legend, & romance.*
44. https://www.duchas.ie, CBÉS 0771, p. 105
45. Houlihan, *Irish Fairies.*
46. https://www.duchas.ie, CBÉ, 0367, p. 140.
47. Mac Cana, *Celtic Mythology.*
48. *Ibid.*
49. Ó hÓgáin, *Myth, legend, & romance.*
50. *Ibid.*
51. *Ibid.*
52. https://www.duchas.ie, CBÉS 0367, p. 140
53. MacCulloch, *Religion of the ancient Celts.*
54. Ó hÓgáin, *Myth, legend, & romance.*
55. Early Irish Glossaries Database (available online at: http://www.asnc.cam.ac.uk/irish glossaries
56. Ó hÓgáin, *The sacred isle.*
57. Ó hÓgáin, *The Lore of Ireland.*

58. *Ibid.*
59. Ross, *Everyday life of the pagan Celts.*
60. Ó hÓgáin, *The Lore of Ireland.*
61. Ross, *Everyday life of the pagan Celts.*
62. Ó hÓgáin, *The Lore of Ireland.*
63. Condron, *The Serpent and the Goddess.*
64. Wentz, *The Fairy-faith in Celtic countries.*
65. https://www.duchas.ie, CBÉS 0600, p. 042.
66. https://www.duchas.ie, CBÉS, 0395, p. 009
67. Gimbutas, *The Living Goddesses.*
68. Ó hÓgáin, *The Lore of Ireland.*
69. Ellis P., *The Druids* (Constable, 1994)
70. *Ibid.*
71. *Ibid.*
72. Green, *Celtic Myths.*
73. Cunliffe, B., *The ancient celts* (Oxford University Press, 2018).
74. Ó hÓgáin, *Myth, legend, & romance.*
75. *Ibid.*
76. Condron, *The Serpent and the Goddess.*
77. Ross, *Everyday life of the pagan Celts.*
78. https://www.duchas.ie, CBÉS 0131C, p. 06_031.
79. Wright, *Brigid: goddess, druidess and saint*
80. MacCulloch, *Religion of the ancient Celts.*
81. MacKillop, *A dictionary of Celtic mythology.*
82. Green, *Celtic Myths.*
83. Ó hÓgáin, *The sacred isle.*
84. Ross, *Everyday life of the pagan Celts.*
85. *Ibid.*
86. https://www.duchas.ie, CBÉS 0845, p. 203.
87. Houlihan, *Irish Fairies.*
88. Wright, *Brigid:goddess, druidess and saint.*
89. https://www.duchas.ie, CBÉS 0182, p. 291.
90. https://www.duchas.ie, CBÉS 0307, p. 134.

Places of the Otherworld
1. Kenny, J., *The Hills Speak, history and mystery* (Dbee Press, 2016).
2. Kelly, *Brigid: Pagan Goddess and Christian Saint.* Irish Lives Remembered, 53, pp. 82–96.

3. Ó hÓgáin, D., *Historic Ireland, 5000 Years of Ireland's Heritage* (Salamander Books Ltd., 2001).
4. https://www.irishtribes.com ailt-articles/irish-language-gaelic/battle-of-allen-as-a-window-on-early-christian-ireland
5. Logan, P., *The holy wells of Ireland* (Colin Smythe, 1981).
6. Kelly, *Brigid: Pagan Goddess and Christian Saint*.
7. Magan, *Listen to the land speak*.
8. Kenny, *The Hills Speak*.
9. Magan, *Listen to the land speak*.
10. Kissane, *Saint Brigid of Kildare*.
11. IFC 905,108.
12. Kenny, *The Hills Speak*.
13. Magan, *Listen to the land speak*.
14. O'Laverty, 'Newgrange Still Called by Its Ancient Name Brugh-Na-Boinne'.
15. BCE stands for Before the Common/Current Era. CE stands for Common/current Era – they are secular or non-religious alternatives to bc and AD.
16. Ó hÓgáin, *Historic Ireland*
17. Kelly, *Brigid: Pagan Goddess and Christian Saint*.

Connecting with Brigit
1. https://www.duchas.ie, CBÉS 0102, p. 181
2. https://www.duchas.ie,CBÉS 0099, p. 027.
3. https://www.duchas.ie,CBÉS 0115, p. 190.
4. https://www.duchas.ie, CBÉS 0973, p. 223.
5. https://www.duchas.ie, CBÉS 0979, p. 180.
6. Ó Duinn, *Where three streams meet*.
7. Ó Duinn, *The Rites of Brigid, Goddess & Saint*.

BIBLIOGRAPHY

Aldhouse-Green, M.J., *Dictionary of Celtic myth and legend.* Thames and Hudson, 1992.

Anonymous, *Cath Maige Tuired: The Second Battle of Mag Tuired.* Translated by Elizabeth A. Gray. CELT: The Corpus of Electronic Texts at University College Cork, T300010. https://celt.ucc.ie/published/T300010/index.html.

Anonymous, 'The Curragh of Kildare', *The Dublin Builder*, 15 May 1866, issue 8. British Newspaper Archive (subscription), accessed 27 December 2024-via British Archive.

Apffel-Marglin, F., *Subversive spiritualities: How rituals enact the world.* OUP, 2011

Ballard, L.M., *The Good People: New Fairylore Essays.* University Press of Kentucky, 1991.

Bethu Brigte, author unknown, https://celt.ucc.ie/published/T201002 (CELT (Corpus of Electronic Texts, a project of University College Cork).

Bourke, A., *Working and Weeping: Women's Oral Poetry in Irish and Scottish Gaelic.* UCD, School of Social Justice, Women's Studies, 1988.

Breen, P., *Pagan Portals-Maman Brigitte: Dark Goddess of Africa and Ireland.* John Hunt Publishing, 2024

Briggs, K.M., *The fairies in tradition and literature.* Psychology Press, 2002.

Byrne, F.J., *Irish kings and high-kings.* Batsford, 1973.

Cambrensis, G., *Expugnatio Hibernica: Conquest of Ireland* (A. B. Scott & F. X. Martin, Eds; Vol. 3). Royal Irish Academy 1978; http://www.jstor.org/stable/j.ctt1p6qp8j

Carmody, I., *The Dagda and the Mór Rígain,* 2018. Retrieved from https://www.academia.edu/42767242/The_Dagda_and_the_Mór_Rigain_in_Cath_Maige_Tuired_from_Harp_Club_and_Cauldron

'Cogitosus; *Life of St Brigid:* content and value' [includes translation of the Life of Cogitosus by S. Connolly and Jean-Michel Picard], *JRSAI*, 1987.

Condit, Tom, and Gabriel Cooney. 'Heritage Guide No. 8: Newgrange, Co. Meath: Neolithic Religion and the

Mid- winter Sunrise', *Archaeology Ireland*, 1999. *JSTOR*, http://www.jstor.org/stable/45128581. Accessed 16 Feb. 2025.

Condren, M., *The Serpent and the Goddess: Women, Religion, and Power in Celtic Ireland*. Harper and Row, 1989.

Connolly, S., *Vita Prima Sanctae Brigitae Background and Historical Value*. The Journal of the Royal Society of Antiquaries of Ireland, vol. 119, JSTOR, 1989

Croker, T.C., *Fairy legends and traditions of the south of Ireland*. William Tegg, 1862.

Cunliffe, B., *The ancient Celts*. Oxford University Press, 2018

Cusack, Carole, 'Brigit: Goddess, Saint, "Holy Woman", and Bone of Contention', *Sydney Studies in Religion*, 2007.

Daimler, M., *Pagan Portals-The Dagda: Meeting the Good God of Ireland*. John Hunt Publishing, 2018.

Daimler, M., *Pagan Portals-Fairy Queens: Meeting The Queens Of The Otherworld*. John Hunt Publishing, 2019

Daimler, M., *Pagan Portals-Aos Sidhe: Meeting the Irish Fair Folk*. John Hunt Publishing, 2022.

Danaher, K., *In Ireland Long Ago*. Mercier Press, 1964

Dinneen, P.S., *An Irish-English Dictionary: Being a Thesaurus of Words, Phrases and Idioms of the Modern Irish Language, with Explanations in English*. For the Irish texts society by MH Gill & son Limited, 1904.

Ellis P., *The Druids*. Constable & Robinson, 1994

Fagan, Brian, 'Timelines: Neolithic Newgrange', *Archaeology*, vol. 47, no. 5, 1994, pp. 16–17, *JSTOR*, http://www.jstor.org/stable/41766471. Accessed 16 Feb. 2025

Farrelly, J., *Farrelly's Field Guide to Irish Faerie Folk*. O'Brien Press, 2024.

Fraser, J., *The first battle of Moytura*. Royal Irish Academy, 1916.

Freeman, P., 2019, January. The Life of Saint *Brigid* by Cogitosus, In *Proceedings of the Harvard Celtic Colloquium*, 2019, The Department of Celtic Languages and Literatures, Faculty of Arts and Sciences, Harvard University.

Freeman, P., *Two Lives of Saint Brigid*, Four Courts Press, 2024

Gimbutas, M., *The living goddesses*. Univ. of California Press, 2001.

Green, M.J., *Celtic myths*. University of Texas Press, 1993.

Gregory, L., *Gods And Fighting Men: The Story of the Tuatha De*

Danaan and of the Fianna of Ireland, arranged and put into English, BoD–Books on Demand, 2024.

Gregory, Lady A. (Revised edition). *Irish Myths and Legends*. New Island Books, 2024.

Harbison, P., *Pre-Christian Ireland: From the First Settlers to the Early Celts*. Thames and Hudson, 1988.

Heaney, M., 'Over Nine Waves: A Book of Irish Legends: The Reign of Bres', *Harvard Review* (6), 1994.

Houlihan, M., *Irish Fairies: A Short History of the Sídhe*. Independently published, 2022.

https//: Brig and Rúadán – Story Archaeology

https://dúchas.ie | National Folklore Collection UCD Digitization Project

https://www.heritagecouncil.ie/content/files/Holy-Wells-of-Ireland.pdf accessed 28/12/24

https://www.joeheaney.org/en/prayer-for-raking-the-fire/

https://www.irishtribes.com/ailt-articles/irish-language-gaelic/battle-of-allen-as-a-window-on-early-christian-ireland

Hutton, R., *Queens of the wild: pagan goddesses in Christian Europe: an investigation*. Yale University Press, 2022.

Irish Sagas: Cath Almaine text, UCC, https://www.iso.ucc.ie/Cath-almaine/Cath-almaine-sources.html – accessed 08/12/24

Kelly, E.P., *The Enchanted Cow in Irish Tradition. Irish Lives Remembered*, 48, digital magazine, produced by Irish Family History Centre (via publisher Eneclann.)

Kelly, E.P., *Brigid: Pagan Goddess and Christian Saint. Irish Lives Remembered*, 53, digital magazine, produced by Irish Family History Centre (via publisher Eneclann.)

Kelly, F., *A guide to early Irish law*, Dublin Institute for Irish Studies, 1988.

Kelly, J., *Battle of Allen as a Window on Early Christian Ireland*, Cló an Druaidh / The Druid Press ; https://www.irishtribes.com/ailt-articles/irish-language-gaelic/battle-of-allen-as-a-window-on-early-christian-ireland. Accessed 28/12/24.

Kenny, J., *The Hills Speak: history and mystery*. Dbee Press, 2016

kildarelocalhistory.ie/articles-Some-local-folk-traditions-relating-to-st. brigid/ accessed 03/01/2024

Kissane, N., *Saint Brigid of Kildare: life, legend and cult*, Open Air, 2017.

Lacey, B., *The Pocket Book of Irish Saints*, O'Brien Press, 2003.

Lawrence, Lisa, 'Pagan Imagery in the Early Lives of Brigit: A Transformation from Goddess to Saint?' *Proceedings of the Harvard Celtic Colloquium*, vol. 16/17, 1996, *JSTOR*, http://www.jstor.org/stable/20557314. Accessed 9 Nov. 2024

Lenihan, E., *In Search of Biddy Early*, HayesPrint Publishing, 2018.

Lenihan, E., *Meeting the Other Crowd*, Gill and Macmillan, 2003.

Livingstone, S., *Scottish customs*, Birlinn Ltd., 2021.

Logan, P., . *The holy wells of Ireland*, Colin Smythe, 1981.

Lysaght, P., *The Banshee: The Irish Supernatural Death-Messenger*, Glendale Press, 1986.

Mac Cana, P., *Celtic Mythology*, Hamlyn, 1970.

MacCulloch, J.A., *Religion of the ancient Celts*. Routledge, 2014.

Mackenzie, D.A., *Wonder Tales from Scottish Myth & Legend*. Blackie and Son, 1917.

MacKillop, J., *A dictionary of Celtic mythology*, Penguin 2006

Magan, M., *Listen to the land speak: A journey into the wisdom of what lies beneath us*, Gill, 2022

McAnally, D.R., *Irish Wonders: The Ghosts, Giants, Pookas, Demons, Leprechauns, Banshees, Fairies, Witches, Widows, Old Maids, and Other Marvels of the Emerald Isle*, Houghton Mifflin, 1888.

McIntyre, M., *The Cailleach Bheara: A Study of Scottish Highland Folklore in Literature and Film*, 2013. Retrieved from https://www.academia.edu / 6088609 _The Cailleach_ Bheara: A_Study_of_Scottish_Highland_Folklore_in_ Literature_and_ Film

Metrical Dindsenchas vol 3, poem 3, Boand CELT) (Corpus of Electronic Texts, a project of University College Cork)

Micheelsen, A., 'King and Druid', in *Proceedings of the Harvard Celtic Colloquium*, Dept of Celtic Languages and Literatures, Faculty of Arts and Sciences, Harvard University, 2000.

Monaghan, P., *The Red-Haired Girl from the Bog: The Landscape of Celtic Myth and Spirit*, New World Library, 2004.

Morris, Henry, 'Where Was Tor Inis, the Island Fortress of the Fomorians?' *The Journal of the Royal Society of Antiquaries of Ireland*, vol. 17, no. 1, 1927, *JSTOR*, http://www.jstor.org/stable/25513429. Accessed 10 May 2024

Murphy, G., The lament of the old woman of Beare. *Proceedings of the Royal Irish Academy. Section C: Archaeology, Celtic Studies, History, Linguistics, Literature*, 55, 1952.

Ó Crualaoich, G., *The Book of The Cailleach*, Cork University Press, 2006.

Ó Duinn, S., *The Rites of Brigid: Goddess and Saint*, Columba Press, 2005.

Ó Duinn, S., *Where three streams meet: Celtic spirituality*. Columba Press, 2000.

O hÓgain, D., *The Lore of Ireland*, Collins Press, 2006.

Ó hÓgáin, D., *Myth, legend, & romance: an encyclopædia of the Irish folk tradition*, Ryan, 1990.

Ó hÓgáin, D., *The sacred isle: belief and religion in pre-Christian Ireland*, Boydell Press, 1999.

Ó hÓgáin, D., *Historic Ireland, 5,000 Years of Ireland's Heritage*, Salamander Books Ltd., 2001.

O'Brien, L., *Fairy Faith in Ireland*. Eel and Otter Press, 2021.

O'Laverty, James, 'Newgrange Still Called by Its Ancient Name, Brugh-Na-Boinne', *The Journal of the Royal Society of Antiquaries of Ireland*, vol. 2, no. 4, 1892, *JSTOR*, http://www.jstor.org/stable/25507944. Accessed 17 Feb. 2025.

Ray, Celeste, 'Paying the Rounds at Ireland's Holy Wells', *Anthropos*, vol. 110, no. 2, 2015, *JSTOR*, http://www.jstor.org/stable/43861969. Accessed 9 Nov. 2024.

'River Boyne: Waters of Wisdom', *Archaeology Ireland*, vol. 11, no. 3, 1997, *JSTOR*, http://www.jstor.org/stable/20558726. Accessed 17 Feb. 2025.

Ross, A., *Everyday life of the pagan Celts*. Batsford, 1970.

Ross, A., *Pagan Celtic Britain: studies in iconography and tradition*. Constable, 1993.

Sjoestedt, M.L., *Celtic Gods and Heroes*, Courier Corporation, 2000.

Stokes (2004), (2010). *The Second Battle of Moytura* Text T300011, CELT (Corpus of Electronic Texts, a project of University College Cork)

Stokes (2001), (2008) *On the Life of Saint Brigid*, Text T201010, CELT (Corpus of Electronic Texts, a project of University College Cork).

Stokes, Whitley (ed. & tr), *The Battle of Allen*, Medieval Irish text and English translation, *Revue Celtique, 24*, 1903; Digital

Edition at Archive.com – accessed November 2024.

The Boyhood Deeds of Fionn mac Cumhaill / www.ancienttexts.org Laud 610.

van Hamel, A.G. ed., *Immrama* (Vol. 10), Dublin Institute for Advanced Studies, 1941

Vučković, A., *Dagda, Potbellied Chief Deity of the Celtic Pantheon.* 2019. Retrieved from www.ancientorigins.net.

Walker, Stephanie Kirkwood, 'Brigit of Kildare as She Is: A Study of Biographical Image', *Biography*, vol. 17, no. 2, 1994, *JSTOR*, http://www.jstor.org/stable/23539666. Accessed 11 Nov. 2024.

Warmind, Morten and Warmind, M Morton, 'Sacred kingship among the Celts', in *Proceedings of the Harvard Celtic Colloquium 12* (1992), Dept of Celtic Languages and Literatures, Faculty of Arts and Sciences, Harvard University, 1992; http://www.jstor.org/stable/20557246. Accessed from JSTOR.

Weber, C., *Brigid: History, Mystery, and Magick of the Celtic Goddess*, Weiser Books, 2015.

Wentz, W.E., *The Fairy-faith in Celtic countries*, H Frowde, 1966.

White, C., *A history of Irish fairies*, Mercier Press, 1976.

Who is the Irish God of Death? The Irish Pagan School, accessed 06/12/24.

Wilde, L., *Ancient Legends of Ireland*. Hobby Horse, 1887.

Wolf, C. and Minard, A., *The Mythical Pairing of Brig and Bres – Its Origin and Meaning in Cath Maige Tuired*, 2015. Retrieved from Casey June Wolf (Mael Brigde) – Academia.edu

Wright, B., *Brigid: goddess, druidess and saint*, The History Press, 2011.

About the Author

Pauline Breen is a devotee of Brigit. She holds a B.A and M.A. in modern languages. Pauline lives in the Irish Midlands and is the author of *This is Brigid – Goddess & Saint of Ireland*, *Maman Brigitte* (Moon Books) and *Brigantia* (Moon Books)